## 'You're Hug

'I am. There's a chair.... ...
down before you fall down.'

'I'm in no danger of falling down.' All the
same, Petra was extremely surprised, to put it
mildly, and she did go so far as to perch on the
edge of the chair. 'Then you're——' She had
been going to say 'Mrs Baron's son', but he beat
her to it.

'The "stuffed shirt"—wasn't that it?' he said.

**Dear Reader**

The background in which a novel is set can be very important to a reader's enjoyment of the story. What type of background do you most enjoy? Do you like a story set in a large international city or do you prefer your story to be set in a quiet rural village away from the hustle and bustle of everyday life? What about exotic locations with hot climates and steamy lifestyles? Let us know and we'll do all we can to get you the story you want!

*The Editor*

**Alison York** was born near Yorkshire's Moors and Dales but now lives in Warwickshire. A French graduate, she has two daughters and a son, all married, and two Siamese cats. She loves writing for the opportunity it offers to explore feelings and motivations. As well as novels, she writes short stories and poems. She is an avid reader—hell for her would have no books—and she also enjoys walking, gardening, theatre, music and art—other people's.

**Recent titles by the same author:**

DISTANT SHADOWS

# TOMORROW'S HARVEST

## BY

## ALISON YORK

**MILLS & BOON LIMITED**
ETON HOUSE   18-24 PARADISE ROAD
RICHMOND   SURREY   TW9 1SR

*First published in Great Britain 1992
by Mills & Boon Limited*

© Alison York 1992

*Australian copyright 1992
Philippine copyright 1992
This edition 1992*

ISBN 0 263 77731 6

92C 1191 T

*Set in Times Roman 10 on 11½ pt.
01-9209-54651 C*

*Made and printed in Great Britain*

# CHAPTER ONE

SIDE by side on the parking space in front of the elegant Georgian-style shops of Granville Row, the two vehicles could not have been less alike. One of them was a gimmicky mock-up of an early delivery van, boxy and dinky, and full of chirpy character. It had a customised trade-name, COLLECTIONS, on each of its sides in elaborate italic script surrounded by a burst of multi-coloured stars. Its neighbour was an opulent silver-grey Rolls with gleaming chrome and immaculately shining windows. The traditional streamlined silver lady on the front of its bonnet looked as though she would rather like to cringe at being in such unworthy company.

The girl getting out of the little van was as individual as her vehicle. She looked to be in her early twenties and had a cloud of dark, rebellious hair and laughing blue eyes. Her Mexican print skirt was almost ankle-length, but showed an intriguing glimpse of black buttoned boots with Louis heels, and the fringes of her black woollen wrap blew in the October wind as she went round to open up the back of the van.

She had just balanced a motley collection of objects in her arms, crowned by an open box, and was bumping the doors of the van to with a saucy movement of her hips when a more conventional trio emerged from the classy-looking antiques shop in the centre of the row.

Leading the trio was the obvious chauffeur of the Rolls, his uniform as discreet and silver-grey as the car. He was carrying a circular mahogany pie-crust table, holding it ceremonially aloft, and he winked at the girl as he passed her. She gave him a quick smile, not averse to a friendly wink, and feeling that it proved that the Rolls hadn't got too much into his blood.

At a much slower pace there followed an elderly lady on the arm of a tall, dark-suited man of the kind of looks and build that merited a second glance. Rugged but remote, the girl thought after a quick assessment. More of the Rolls in *his* blood, without a doubt.

The pair had reached the edge of the pavement when the box crowning the girl's load slipped and tilted over sideways, spilling out a shower of marbles which shot off in all directions.

'Oh—d...ear!' she exclaimed with what she considered remarkable instant self-control. She dumped her load on the pavement and flung herself after the marbles, calling an impassioned 'Stop that Chinaman going down the drain, will you?' to whoever was willing to help.

With hardly a split second's hesitation, Mr Rugged but Remote realised that the Chinaman was the ceramic marble with the black and white bands, and shot out a foot to stop it. Then, with a quiet, 'Just a second, Mrs Willoughby. Wait here, will you? I don't want you to fall,' he crouched down and helped to collect the rest of the spillage. The chauffeur, the table safely stowed in the boot of the Rolls, joined in, highly amused.

'How about a game while we're down here?' he said quietly to the girl out of the corner of his mouth.

'Not much chance of a three-hander!' she said with a humorous glance at the face of the third collector.

At that moment, he stood and came towards her. 'No more, as far as I can see,' he said coldly, dropping his findings into the box.

She thanked him with a dazzling smile. 'Clever of you to realise which was the Chinaman. I'd hate to lose that— it's the only one I've got. Plenty of Aggies and Water

Babies and Puries. Even quite a few Cat's Eyes and Blood Alleys. But only one Chinaman.'

'Then you'd better take more care of him,' the man said shortly, and with a cool nod he turned to offer his arm to the patiently waiting elderly lady.

'I'm sorry to have held you up,' the girl said to her in quick apology.

The old lady smiled. 'Quite a diversion—and it took me back years. I used to play marbles with my brother much longer ago than I care to remember. He always won. As a matter of fact I used to wear boots like yours too! Fancy that style coming back!'

The girl held out a neat ankle and twirled her foot. 'These are genuine antiques, and have hardly been worn at all. Quite a find. I love all the buttons—didn't you? Can't put them on in a hurry, though.'

'You didn't do anything in a hurry in those days,' the old lady smiled. She looked up into the stern face of her escort. 'One never knows what one will encounter on a visit to Granville Antiques, Hugo.'

'Quite.' For a moment as he looked down at her genuine warmth flickered in his grey-green eyes and the rather forbidding mouth softened. 'We do, on the whole, though, try not to link pie-crust tables with booby traps. Let me help you across to the car.'

So he didn't belong to the Rolls, not this particular one, anyway. The antiques shop was his domain. As they moved across the lay-by to the Rolls his eyes met the girl's again, and the shutters went down on the momentary warmth he had shown.

All right, Mr Double R, the girl thought. You couldn't put it more clearly. I'm not your kind of person. Not old enough, not rare enough, and not a trace of genuine pie-crust about me. See if I care. There's room for both of us on Granville Row.

She stooped to pick up her load then thought better of it and went over to unlock the door of the next shop to Granville Antiques before beginning the balancing act again. She might not care what he thought, but one performance like that was enough, thank you. She came back quickly and scooped up the rest of her things, pausing once inside the shop to look back again at the activities in the lay-by.

The Rolls was moving majestically off, and its neighbour, the little van, was now exposed to the attention of the man from Granville Antiques, who was standing staring at it with an expression of total disbelief on his face. He reminded the girl fleetingly of Oscar Wilde's Lady Bracknell in the split second before she thundered, 'A *handbag*?'

She smothered another smile and ducked away from the window before he turned and saw her watching him. Her blue eyes concentrated on the shop's interior and she smiled with pleasure.

'A roof over my head!' she murmured. 'Fancy that!' She wandered around, opening the door at the back and looking through into the little kitchen. Just before it there was another door concealing a staircase, and she ran up excitedly to the second floor. All this space! After selling her bygones from a stall at the top end of the scale and a car boot at the bottom, this was luxury indeed. Not long-lived luxury, since she only had the shop until the end of January, but something to be savoured while it lasted.

She went downstairs again. The shop was carpeted in red. There was dark shelving on one wall—that would be useful. The velvet-draped curtained cubicles—it must have been a dress shop—could be arranged as theme areas with the curtains as backcloth on which to pin small objects. She stood, lost in thought for a while, planning and arranging in her mind. The window was low and had spotlighting over its display area. She could do a lot with that.

Through the window she could see that one of the van doors had swung slightly open again, a reminder to quit staring and get on with the unloading she was here to do. She took off her wrap, pushed up the sleeves of her red jumper, and set to work.

Some time later she had carried everything in and deposited it anyhow along the sides of the shop, and was just beginning to get to grips with how she would arrange it all when she realised that someone was looking in the window—the man from the antiques shop, his strong face lit in the glow from the window lights which she had switched on to try them. He was looking down at the motley collection of objects she had dumped there—a box of iron keys, another of copper jelly moulds, a Chinese vase, a watering can in brass and copper, and an umbrella stand. A bumper frown was establishing itself over the man's dark eyebrows. He did not appear to like what he was seeing and the ten or so years' advantage he had over her was probably making him think he had a right to convey his opinion. He looked up and met her eyes, pointed to the door, and indicated brusquely that he wished to come in. He didn't look as though he contemplated a refusal.

The girl gave a cheerful nod and beckoning sign, calling, 'It's open.'

As he came through the door his foot caught against a gloriously vulgar Victorian chamberpot, full-blown roses on the outside, a huge eye winking up from the bottom of the inside. There was a loud, melodious clang as foot and china made contact.

'Shows it's not cracked,' the girl said cheerfully, unabashed, moving it to one side with her quaint buttoned boot. 'Hello again. I'm Petra Collins.' She held out a hand, small, but with long, slender fingers, and still sporting a summer tan so that it managed to look both delicate and businesslike at the same time.

The man took it, dwarfing it briefly in his own hand.

'Granville Antiques, as I think you already know.'

And nameless, apparently. Well, if that was the way he wanted things, so be it. Petra remained cheerful and smiling.

'Sorry about the business with the marbles. It didn't seem to put your lady off, fortunately.'

He was not disposed to rehash the earlier incident.

'Is that your van out there?'

'Yes. I presume it's all right to leave it there? There were no parking restrictions that I could see.'

'There are none. But we do tend to leave our own transport round the back and make room for customers in the lay-by. And since yours is a commercial vehicle...'

'You'll have to point out a dark corner for me to hide it in,' Petra said sunnily.

He walked a couple of paces along the shop, not too happily preoccupied with what he was seeing.

'Is this what "Collections" refers to?' he asked abruptly.

Admittedly, piled higgledy-piggledy in shabby cardboard boxes or lying anyhow on the floor, it was not an impressive sight. But Petra loved her bygones and was ready to defend them. Her chin rose determinedly.

'It is. "Collections" as in things people just love to collect.'

'You sell second-hand——' He had been going to say 'rubbish', she knew he had, but he caught himself just in time and said, 'Things'.

'As you do.'

A flicker of the grey-green eyes showed that her quick answer had gone home. 'Hardly a reasonable comparison.'

'Why not? Your stock has belonged to someone else, as mine has.'

He looked out at the van again. 'I was under the impression that "Collections" referred to clothes. Designer collections.'

'I sell clothes too.' She fished a twenties bead-fringed dress out of a box behind her, held it up against herself and did a quick Charleston step or two. 'Beautiful, isn't it? See how the fringe catches the light.'

He exhaled irritably. 'Look—I think there must have been some mistake. This is intended to be a ladies' clothes shop. A high-class clothes shop. You have only to look around you at the fittings to see that.'

'Yes, but it doesn't matter. It will suit me very well. I'm ever so adaptable.'

He seemed to grow even taller. 'I wasn't thinking so much about whether the shop would do for you. It's more a matter of whether your business will do for the shop. For *this* shop in the middle of *this* row of shops.'

Petra's eyes glittered dangerously. 'Are you saying that I'll lower the tone?'

'Put like that it sounds rather offensive.'

'It *is* rather offensive,' she said levelly.

He picked up the Haw's watering can in the window, momentarily distracted. 'I've got one of these at my place. Belonged to my grandfather. They go on for ever.'

'And surely that means quality?' Petra asked pointedly.

He put the can down. 'I think you'd better come outside if you can spare a moment. There's something I'd like to show you.'

She looked at him, weighing what he was up to, then deciding that it might be entertaining to find out. 'As long as it *is* only for a moment.'

'It won't take long.'

Petra moved towards her wrap. He reached out and picked it up. There were obviously good manners there, even to inferiors, she thought, tongue-in-cheek. He turned the wrap round in his hands, mystified as to how it worked.

'Like this.' Petra took it from him, swung it over her back, then tossed the right front panel over her left shoulder. 'Easy when you know how. So where are we going?'

He held the door open, handing her the key from the inside of the lock. 'I'm going to show you the rest of the Row.'

'How kind of you,' Petra said ironically as she passed him and turned to lock the door.

Beyond her temporary premises there was a rare-books shop with one or two tooled leather beauties flanking a stunning illuminated volume displayed on black silk in the window. Then came a chemist's, only they called it a pharmacy, and the windows didn't display cheap, cheerful cosmetics and indiscreet remedies, but jewel-coloured apothecaries' jars. Smythe-Williams, Tailor, next in line, offered a mahogany and wine velvet setting for one superior and no doubt highly costly suit. Beyond the tailor's was the opaque, gilt-bordered window of Roberts, Hunt and Deacon, Solicitors.

'Very nice,' Petra said cheerfully, smiling brightly up at her escort.

Beyond Granville Antiques in the reverse direction was a beauty salon, all white satin and gold-topped jars against gilded screens. Then came a delicatessen with a display of rare cheeses and exotic pâtés on straw mats against a backdrop of real-looking grasses and dried flowers. The double windows were more like still-lifes than a commercial display. Last was a hairdresser, only the Simone in question called herself a *coiffeuse*, and no doubt her prices matched her pretentiousness.

And slap in the middle of all that opulent respectability there's me—bag-lady *par excellence*! Petra thought, sorely tempted to break out laughing.

As they reached Granville Antiques again, she found herself being ushered through its door into the thickly carpeted, hushed interior.

'There'll be tea waiting in the office,' Mr Double R said. 'We can talk while we drink it.'

'Does anything need to be said?' Petra asked, not really expecting an answer and not getting one.

There was a tasteful display of beautiful old furniture in the shop, and it was well arranged with plenty of space to show it off, giving the effect of a home rather than business premises. She turned over the ticket on a delicate little secretaire as they passed. The price was coded. 'So high-class that money is scarcely mentioned,' she observed naughtily.

'Just the system we've always used. Milk or lemon?' he asked.

Petra looked at the tray on the desk in his office. Did people really still say that these days? In his world they obviously did. The tray had a pristine lace cloth. On a silver dish were neatly arranged *langue-de-chat* biscuits. She requested lemon, and took a biscuit to nibble with appropriate daintiness.

'So—you've seen the Row,' he said, putting sugar into his tea.

'And I've got the message—but I'm quite unmoved by it.'

His frown reappeared momentarily, then was smoothed out.

'Tell me, how did you come to receive the offer of the premises next door?' he asked. 'All I know is that it was through Mrs Baron.' Another quick frown. Thoughts of the generous but non-discriminating Mrs Baron obviously gave him no pleasure at all.

Petra launched into a justification of her rights to the shop next door. 'Mrs Baron was certainly my good fairy. She came to a collectors' fair where I had a stand. It was in a pub the other side of Cheltenham. My stand was in the second room at the foot of a small flight of steps, and it was getting on for packing-up time when this elegant grey-haired lady fell headlong down the steps, doing her ankle no good at all. She told me when she'd come round from the shock that she'd been looking at a silvered baby's shoe on my stall instead of watching her step.'

'How unnecessary!' he intervened forcefully. 'If she was old enough for grey hair she should have had her mind on what she was doing.'

'She said she'd had a baby's shoe like that one, once, belonging to her son. But it had been stolen along with other things. She tends to keep looking for it, apparently, whenever she's at a collectors' fair. That's the thing about my collections, you see. They may not come up to yours for intrinsic worth, but they have loads of sentimental value.'

She darted a look at him, long dark lashes screening mischievous blue eyes. He was stirring his tea absentmindedly.

'And was it the one? The shoe she'd lost?' he asked abruptly.

'No, unfortunately. There was a hole in the toe of her little boy's, which made it easy to identify. Apparently this son was a very determined child. He used to kick and kick against the floor with that particular foot in sheer impatience while he was waiting to be taken anywhere. Better the floor than people, though, Mrs Baron said.'

'Oh, good grief! What rubbish!' The china cup went down on his desk with a resounding rattle, spilling tea into the saucer.

'I thought it was rather sweet.' Petra smiled at him. 'She said she would desperately like to get that shoe back, anyway.'

'What on earth for? She's an old lady, and by the same token her son's obviously a mature adult.'

'She wants it as a memory-jogger. She told me that her son is becoming a stuffed shirt these days. She really needs it to remind herself that he was once rather sweet.'

'And for that ridiculous reason she falls headlong down steps and creates mayhem. Then—no doubt suffering from concussion—she goes giving away shop leases like a crazy woman.'

'Not quite,' Petra said firmly. 'I packed up early and took her home to her flat and made her some tea. Her ankle was all right once the initial pain had worn off, but she was glad of company for a bit. She said that with a son like hers you built up a terrible need to talk to someone every so often, poor old thing. It was several days later that she wrote and offered me the tail-end of next door's lease. I found it hard to believe too, but it certainly wasn't an action dreamed up in a state of concussion. And the lease is legal and watertight. A friend checked it for me.'

The dark brows had gathered ominously over the cold green eyes again.

'And you didn't hesitate about the appropriateness of the gesture? You hadn't exactly done a lot, had you?'

'Hesitate? Me?' Petra's blue eyes widened in innocent-seeming surprise. 'Heavens, no. Seize the moment, that's my motto.'

'You don't feel that an impartial observer could think you are taking advantage of an elderly lady who made an exaggerated response to a fairly routine kindness?'

Petra decided she had had enough. Her slim frame tensed and she looked direct defiance at him. 'I hardly put you in the category of impartial observer. And if you are implying that I took advantage of a lady who is not in her right mind, then you don't know Mrs Baron.' She stood, looking at her watch. 'I have no more time, and certainly precious little inclination to go on talking. I'm expecting friends with more things for the shop.' She made for the door, but stopped opposite his desk. 'And, just so that the offensiveness isn't all on one side, I don't really think that my business is any of your damned business. So thank you for the tea. Thank you for the tour. Now I'll get on with my work. And you, Mr Granville Antiques, since you haven't done me the courtesy of offering your name, will have to do the proverbial thing and like it or lump it. Good afternoon.'

With heightened colour but no loss of dignity she walked out of the office, surprising an amused smile that discretion quickly wiped off the face of a secretary waiting to go into the office.

Outside, she saw that Joe and Manda had arrived and were sitting patiently in the front of Joe's Gardening Services van, waiting for her to show up.

'Sorry to keep you waiting,' Petra said as they got out.

'Getting friendly with the neighbours?' Manda asked.

'You're joking! This one's never heard of friendship. He stopped short of setting the dogs on me, but only just.'

Joe looked with interest at Granville Antiques. 'What on earth's bugging him? He didn't waste much time.'

'He doesn't think my trade will add anything to the glamour of the Row. Thinks I'm not from the right social drawer. Mr and Mrs Average can actually afford what I sell. That's bad news around here.'

'Is that him?' Manda asked with sudden interest.

The Granville Antiques man was coming out to look at the far window of his frontage, gesturing to someone inside, who was obviously moving furniture to order.

'For heaven's sake don't let him see you staring. I've had enough of him for one day.' Petra hurriedly opened the door and pushed them inside.

'Public school. You can see it written all over him,' Manda said, squinting through the window.

'Doesn't get his suits from your old high-street shops either, does he?' Joe observed.

'I could tick off the things that go to make him on three fingers,' Petra said, pulling a mocking face. 'Basic clay moulded by Eton or some such rarefied atmosphere. Packaging by Savile Row. And finally—a fair old input from a refrigeration plant.'

Manda grinned. 'Sounds like a bit of a challenge for you.'

'He'll find me a bit of a challenge for him, too,' Petra said firmly. 'But that's enough about that. What do you think?' She gestured proudly round the shop. 'Not bad, eh? One up on previous settings, don't you think?'

'Incredible!' They wandered around admiring and exclaiming, upstairs and out in the kitchen, then back into the main room.

'Well, we've had the grand tour—and very grand indeed it is. Now I guess we'd better get on with the unloading,' Joe said.

Petra hesitated, then said apologetically, 'There's just one problem, I'm sorry to say. The trestle-tables you've brought are obviously out for a place like this. I should have realised before.'

'Ha! He's got to you!' Manda taunted.

'Rubbish. But the place sets its own standards without help from anyone. I've been thinking that it will be far better to use Aunt Jess's little tables and group things on them in themes. Can you bear to go back and swap the load?'

'Since it's you. But what are you going to do without tables at home? You've such a lot of bits and pieces to find homes for there,' Manda said.

'I'll have a ferret around in the attic. It's crammed with stuff. I'm sure to find others that will do me up there, but they'll need cleaning and I want to get this place sorted out quickly.'

'You want to show Mr Next Door a thing or two!'

'Maybe I do. Wouldn't you?'

'OK. We're off, then. Sure you want the whole lot brought?'

'Please. And if you grab some coffee and milk and sugar from my kitchen we can brew up when we feel like it. There's a kettle in the back and I've got cups in one of these boxes.'

'I'll do better than that,' Joe told her. 'I'll bring a bottle of plonk. That'll wash the nasty taste of your neighbour away.'

'Joe, you're a darling. Why didn't I marry you?'

'Because I got him first. Come on, spouse. See you later, Petra,' Manda said.

It was growing dark outside in Granville Row by the time the tables were unloaded. Joe and Manda were through in the kitchen opening the bottle of Asti and pouring it into three cups since the only glasses were Victorian, tiny and fragile. Petra was trying different positions for the tables when the door opened and the man from the antiques shop walked in.

'I hadn't said all I wanted to say when you rushed off for your appointment,' he said.

Petra eyed him across a sofa table. 'I can't think what else there can be to add, unless you feel like tacking on an apology.'

He looked frostily at her. 'Do you have to be so confrontational?'

'After your idea of a welcome, I think I do.'

As they faced each other, Petra became aware of the laughter issuing from the kitchen. There was a loud, unmistakable popping sound and a shriek from Manda. 'My frock! Quick! In the cup!'

The antiques man's face congealed a little more. 'I didn't realise you were not alone.'

Joe and Manda chose that moment to burst through the kitchen door, bearing cups.

'Oh, sorry. I didn't hear anyone come in,' Joe said.

'You're just in time to share the Asti!' Manda said mischievously, knowing full well who the visitor was. A fair amount of the Asti seemed to have gone down her front.

Petra saw them suddenly through the antiques man's grey-green eyes. Joe, sweater and jeans clad and wearing the knee-high leather boots he adopted for gardening work, had an eyepatch over one eye. The reason for it was prosaic—he had walked into the cross-cane of the runner beans, which should have come down weeks ago—but it gave him a wicked, piratical look. Manda was decked in her usual blend of hectic, random-coloured layers with a silver mesh scarf knotted round her forehead, its ends streaming down among her startling but natural red curls. The man from next door would mark them down as hippies, and alcoholic hippies at that.

He ignored the invitation from Manda, confining himself to telling Petra, 'I'd like a private word somewhere.'

'You can have all the words you want right here,' she told him dangerously. 'I have no secrets from Joe and Manda. We live in the same house.' And now make a hippy commune out of that, she added mentally.

He digested this information in silence for a second or two, then said, 'Without wishing to offend your friends——'

Petra didn't allow him to finish. 'For someone who doesn't wish to offend, you have a pretty good stab at it.'

'Er—time to go and look for a top-up, I think,' Joe said good-naturedly, drawing Manda through into the kitchen and firmly closing the door behind them. There was a charged silence while blue eyes locked with green.

'As I was saying,' he continued, 'the best thing we can do is talk this issue over at the Baron Estates office. Can you go over there tomorrow morning?' His eyes ranged over the chaos in the shop. 'Or don't you feel you will be sufficiently in control of things here?'

'Why bother the Barons?' Petra said shortly. 'Mrs Baron would only tell you what I have already told you—that she offered and I accepted a legitimate short-term lease for these premises until the end of January.'

'Mrs Baron might have arranged that. But Mr Baron is involved too.'

'Her husband?'

'No. Her son.'

'The stuffed shirt!'

'If it amuses you to call him that.'

Petra had a rapid debate with herself. She might find it amusing to see the famous kicking son. And in any case somebody had to get it into this hostile neighbour's head that she had had every right to be here and every intention of staying. In fact the intention grew, the more opposed to her he showed himself to be.

'How do you know Mr Baron will be available at such short notice?' she asked.

'He'll be available,' he said grimly. 'Shall we say eleven?'

'You can even dictate the time?' Petra marvelled sweetly.

'Is eleven possible for you?' he queried again with heavy patience.

'Quite suitable for me.'

'In that case, we'll meet there.'

'Unless Mr Baron thinks otherwise.'

He departed without further comment.

Joe and Manda came out from their retreat.

'Wow!' Manda said.

'Wow indeed.' Petra pushed her hair back irritably. 'Why does there have to be a fly in every ointment?' Joe was grinning. 'And what's amusing *you*?' she asked him.

'I was just thinking—nice to have something to look forward to. You'll enjoy tomorrow.'

Petra picked up the pillow on which she displayed her lace bobbins and threw it at him.

'You know what?' she said to Manda. 'This man of yours has a malicious sense of humour. I'm glad you got him.'

They laughed, dispelling a little of the tension the antiques man had brought into the shop, then work became the order of the rest of the day.

Petra found it was not so easy to dismiss thoughts of the man next door, though. The disapproving face with

its critical grey-green eyes seemed to be looking over her
shoulder all the time. When she looked round at the end
of the stint, pleased with the effect the three of them
had achieved, she found herself thinking 'Well, he can't
complain about that if he's a grain of honesty in him.'
Idiot! she added, addressing herself. The shop pleased
her, and that was what mattered. Never mind the
neighbours.

'All set for Monday,' Manda said.

Petra made up her mind. 'I'm not waiting until
Monday, I'm going to open tomorrow if you can stand
in for me at a quarter to eleven when I go to the Baron
Estates' office.' She was pretty sure she could count on
Manda, who sewed and knitted her silk and woollen ex-
travaganzas at home and enjoyed a change of background now and then.

A broad smile was spreading over Manda's face. 'I
can do that. Opening before meeting him should show
the antiques man a thing or two, shouldn't it?'

Petra returned the grin. 'Just what I thought. No harm
in coming out fighting.'

Joe winced. 'The poor man doesn't know what he's
taking on!' he said with feeling.

They switched out the lights and left Granville Row
to its Georgian calm. Petra couldn't help wondering how
long it would last.

# CHAPTER TWO

THE Collections window was framed in witchballs, glowing deep cobalt-blue, green and cranberry as the spotlights caught their fire, and linked by Manda's clever, delicate artificial cobwebs.

A burnished copper jam pan, next best thing to a witch's cauldron, stood centre-window and from it spilled coloured ribbons, each ribbon leading to a different group of objects. Autumn leaves in all their rich colours filled the spaces in between, and towards the front of the window stood the carved wood COLLECTIONS sign, announcing that bygones were bought and sold, and that browsers were welcome.

Petra gave her Hallowe'en display a last proud look as she left for the Baron Estates office, at the same time checking her reflection in the glass of the window. Her long navy-blue cloak and matching cloche hat looked businesslike enough, and her determination was running high. Manda waved a goodbye from inside the shop, and as Petra got into the van, which she had only left in front so that Manda could use the parking space round the back, she saw two women going into Collections. There had been a surprising number of browsers in the one and a half hours since she opened, two of whom had bought. A good sign if ever there was one.

The Baron Estates office was in a courtyard nearer the centre of Cheltenham. Petra was shown into the office where she had previously signed her lease with Mrs Baron. She took one of the chairs facing the desk, and toyed with the idea of slipping off her cloak, since the heating was super-effective, but decided against it. It would give the impression that she was here for a prolonged discussion, which she fervently hoped she was not.

She had arrived early. Mildly curious to see what sort of car the Granville Antiques man drove, she went over to look down into the courtyard in the hope of seeing him turn up, but she had hardly reached the window when he walked into the office.

'Good morning,' Petra said.

'Good morning.' There had been on his face the shadow of the smile he must have given the secretary in the outer office, but once again when he saw Petra it was as though shutters came down inside his head. Somewhere in his brain the 'trouble' sign triggered negative thoughts, and his face was only too good at expressing them.

'I was surprised to see your business in operation this morning,' he said without any further civilities. 'I rather thought you would wait at least until you knew the outcome of today's meeting.'

'I rather thought you would rather think that,' Petra said sardonically.

'It would have made sense. If there is a change of plan after today, you've laid out your wares for nothing.'

'But I don't anticipate a change of plan. I'm here to have you convinced that the original plan was watertight. Did you like the window?' she enquired with bravado.

'I didn't look closely. The general effect was of Christmas—rather too early. And there were cobwebs. Odd. Most people spend all their time trying to ensure that no such things gain ground.'

'That's in honour of Hallowe'en, as are the witchballs.'

'Am I to understand that you dabble in witchcraft?'

'There are certainly times when I have a strong urge to make a wax model of someone and stick pins in it,' she retorted crisply.

For a moment she thought he was going to show amusement, but it came to nothing. 'If you find yourself having to move all the stuff you've scattered around in Granville Row after all my warnings, the only model deserving pins will be one of yourself. I spent a considerable amount of time yesterday trying to convince you that you were out of your element.'

'The only person who could legitimately do that is Mr Baron, and I certainly don't anticipate any such reaction from him.'

He gave her a strange look, then what he said next completely took the wind out of Petra's sails.

'I think it's time I introduced myself. Hugo Baron, joint owner of the Granville Row shops.' He walked round to the big oak and leather chair behind the desk and sat in it, a shadow of smug satisfaction in his eyes at the shock he had only too obviously given her.

'You're Hugo Baron?' she echoed stupidly.

'I am. There's a chair behind you. I should sit down before you fall down.'

'I'm in no danger of falling down.' All the same, Petra was extremely surprised, to put it mildly, and she did go so far as to perch on the edge of the chair. 'Then you're——' She had been going to say 'Mrs Baron's son', but he beat her to it.

'The "stuffed shirt" —wasn't that it?' he said.

A wave of colour washed over Petra's face, but she wasn't going to allow herself to be browbeaten.

'I didn't call you that. Your own mother did.'

'But you were not exactly averse to repeating it.'

'You questioned me about how I came to be given the lease. I answered your questions. And I might say that

I find your underhand approach extremely unattractive. If you had told me at the outset who you were, I would never have repeated that particular remark of your mother's.'

'You needn't worry over-much,' he said grimly. 'I'm quite accustomed to my mother's plain speaking.'

Petra was beginning to realise that there was humour in the situation. 'I see now why you got so shirty about the baby's shoe.' She tried to picture this big, aggressive-looking man with eyes that looked out at the world expecting trouble as a 'sweet' little boy, and found it an impossible feat of imagination. 'You really shouldn't have encouraged me to babble on as you did,' she said.

'I wanted to find out exactly why my mother had arranged this impulsive business. I was away at the time, and all the information she left for me before going away herself was a copy of the lease, and a note saying you had done her a favour and she wanted to give you a helping hand in return.'

Petra looked steadily at him. 'And are you satisfied with what you managed to find out?'

There was a fraction less hostility in his eyes now. 'Satisfied that it was a genuine meeting and not some scheme you'd cooked up. I'm a good enough judge of character to realise that.'

There was silence for a second while Petra digested his words and the way he said them.

'You are *incredible*,' she said at last. 'I really believe that you think that was a pleasant remark, and that I should be glad to hear it.'

'And aren't you?' The strong eyebrows rose questioningly.

'I'm amazed that you should have such a downbeat view of human nature—and such a poor opinion of your own mother's judgement.'

'When someone acts out of character, it pays to question why. My mother has never before gone ahead with a business decision without consulting me. This time she did, and the nature of the deal certainly gave me reason to think she had acted unwisely.'

'Before you had even spoken to me? You came in with all guns blazing from the word go, it seems to me.'

'From the moment I saw the nature of the stock you were taking in, I realised that Granville Row was not the right environment for your sort of trade.'

'But that really is absurd. You're in the same trade, whether you like it or not.'

'That is as ridiculous as saying that painting by numbers is in the same category as producing a Renoir.'

'Not in the least.' Petra's eyes were sparking with anger now. 'My stock may not have the same price-range as yours, but that's due to size and fashionable opinion. I defy you to examine any number of things in my collections and say that pride and skill of workmanship isn't there before your eyes.'

'All the same, Miss Collins, a watering can does not bear comparison with the work of Chippendale, Sheraton, or Hepplewhite.'

'Good workmanship is good workmanship on whatever scale. You are speaking from sheer snobbery.'

'I'm speaking from the point of view of a person who realises that there are standards, and likes to maintain them. I have standards for Granville Row. Your business does not fit into the parameters I have for the shops there. Be realistic. Where do you normally carry on your trade? From the rear of your van on some muddy airfield? From a scruffy trestle-table in a draughty school hall? Such images are linked inevitably with what you sell—and they are not the images I wish to have connected with Granville Row.'

'For three short months?' she exclaimed. 'Will the foundations of Granville Row crumble in that short time?'

'No. But the public view of Granville Row would change, no matter how imperceptibly. I don't intend that to happen.'

Petra leaned back and looked at him almost pityingly.

'What a worrying life you must lead with all these obscure, incomprehensible standards bugging you.' He didn't answer, just sat implacably waiting for her to give in. She got up and went over to the window, conscious of the fact that he was watching her and thinking that perhaps she was on the point of weakening. But Petra never weakened in the face of opposition—rather the reverse. She turned and faced him from across the room. 'You're right, of course, about my usual trading spots. I *do* sell in markets, schools, pubs—anywhere they'll have me. I've never had a shop of my own before...always lived out of boxes. Now I've got this unbelievable opportunity to have three months' consistent trading from one place. Of course I want to take it. Moreover, I have reason to think, on professional advice, that the agreement your mother drew up is legal, and that she had the right to execute it. Now you are expecting me to give up that once-in-a-lifetime chance because you don't like me or my business.'

'I'm not asking you to give it up for nothing. I have other premises I can offer you in a more appropriate place for the same length of time.'

'Is there a sufficiently insalubrious place in this town for someone like me?' Petra asked, her blue eyes widening with mock surprise in which not a little plain anger was mixed.

'I don't really think you expect an answer to a remark like that.' He stood up. 'Why don't you come and see for yourself? That's why I invited you here.' He took a bunch of keys from a drawer in the desk.

Petra thought rapidly. She was fairly sure of her position legally. He hadn't challenged her when she said she considered her agreement with his mother sound, and, in view of the fact that he wanted her out of Granville Row so badly, she was sure that he would have picked her up on that if he had been able to do so. She rather suspected that his mother was the majority share-holder in the business.

So—she could in all likelihood stay on until the end of January. But did she really want to spend three months in an icy atmosphere with a neighbour who was also her extremely hostile landlord? It needed more thought. Going to see the alternative premises would give her time, and set up the option if she wanted to take it.

'All right. I'll look. But I'm saying no more than that at this stage,' she said.

'Fair enough.'

'And if it's not out of our way I'd like to let my stand-in at the shop know that this business is taking longer than anticipated.'

'We go past Granville Row. You can leave your van here.'

He was thinking that they would be coming back here to sign a new contract. You can count your chickens, Mr Baron, dear, Petra thought. But I'm the one controlling the hatching.

Back at Collections, Manda had sales to boast about.

'Two lace bobbins, an inkwell and one of the papier mâché letter racks,' she said proudly. 'And someone's coming back for the Chinese vase when she's measured the niche she'd like it for, all being well.'

'Great!' Petra enthused. 'Listen, though. I haven't finished with our friend next door yet. Can you stay on?'

'All day if you want. No hurry. I've plenty to do. What's causing the hold-up? I thought your Baron friends would have that prickly cactus sorted out in no time.'

'That's the trouble. Not all the Barons come into the category of friends. Too long a story to go into now, but I'll tell you all later. He's waiting out front for me. There are sandwiches in the kitchen if you're getting peckish. I'll get something from the deli, so eat the lot if you want.'

Cloak billowing in the autumn breeze and one hand pinning her cloche to her fly-away hair, Petra ran back to Hugo Baron's car. It wasn't a Rolls, but an Alfa Romeo Cloverleaf. Like the Rolls she had first mistakenly associated with him, though, this car looked as if it would sail majestically through all opposition. But he needn't let that give him ideas about me, Petra thought as she slipped into the sports-style passenger-seat.

He watched as she settled herself and solved the problem offered by cloak and seatbelt.

'Have you got something against the common or garden coat?' he asked.

'Should one be attracted to an "ordinary" anything?' she countered. 'There are so many extraordinary things clamouring for attention. You don't have an "ordinary" car, for instance. You have one with hand-stitched leather trim and electronically operated everything.'

'You really do put all you've got into fighting your corner, don't you?' he said, eyes on the road ahead.

'Don't you think that's rather rich, in view of where we're going and what you're trying to do?'

She glanced sideways at him as she said this and intercepted a glance from him. For the first time there was humour on his face when he looked at her—only slight, but it was there—and the improvement in his appearance was phenomenal.

'Your point, I think,' he said, returning his full attention to the road ahead.

They turned into a small link street between two more important roads, went past an estate agent, a cluster of building societies and a branch bank, then stopped in front of an empty shop. Across the road was a printing works and what looked like a furniture warehouse.

Petra allowed herself to be conducted round the premises in silence, leaving all the talking to Hugo Baron. If she had not seen the Granville Row shop first, she would probably have thought herself extremely lucky to have been offered this place. But Granville Row took a heck of a lot of living up to.

'I appreciate that you were offered Granville Row at a peppercorn rent,' her escort said finally. 'I would be quite prepared to waive any rent at all if you agree to move here.'

Petra's blue eyes looked challengingly at him. 'Trying to buy me off, Mr Baron? That ploy has never worked with me, I can assure you.'

'The amount involved is hardly enough to buy anyone off. I intended only to offer a small concession in view of the inconvenience of packing up and moving again. And I would offer practical help with that, it goes without saying.'

'You really are eager to get rid of me, aren't you?' Petra said, going to the window and looking across at the printer's. 'Well, I'm not saying either yes or no right now. I'll take a little time to think. In the meantime I

realise that you consider you've made me a fair offer.
I'll certainly mull it over.'

He looked at his watch. 'Perhaps you'll allow me to
give you lunch while your subconscious gets to work?'

Petra gave a rueful grin. 'You pull out all the stops,
don't you?'

'I consider it no more than good manners to offer
food to a client when business has run on into the lunch-
hour,' he said shortly. 'If free trading doesn't influence
you, I don't imagine the odd meal will swing the scales.
In any case, the offer's there and the choice is yours.'

'Well, I'm hungry enough, so I'll accept. Thank you
very much.'

'Do you need to make a phone call first?'

'No. Manda isn't in a hurry to go anywhere.'

'What about her own lunch?'

'There's something at the shop for her.'

'Good. Let's be on our way, then.'

So the man in the iron mask has feelings, Petra thought
as they went out to the car. He was kind to old ladies—
admittedly ones from whom he had just made money.
And he gave thought to other people's welfare even while
engaged in plotting to achieve his own ends. His mother
could be right. Perhaps there was a store of niceness
somewhere deep under that stuffed shirt.

Careful! she told herself. Go on like that and you won't
have the heart to refuse the man anything.

She had been thinking hard while they were going
around the shop. If Mrs Baron was as aware of all as-
pects of Baron Estates business as she had given the impression of being, and if she was a woman of usually
sound judgement, as her son said she was, then why had
she offered Petra the Granville Row shop when the one
they had just seen was empty too? She must have known
her son would not approve, and especially she must have

known how he would hate having Petra's *infra dig* business next door to his precious antiques emporium. And yet Mrs Baron had gone ahead and drawn up that lease, before diplomatically withdrawing from the scene and leaving the two protagonists to fight it out.

Petra was now remembering something Mrs Baron had said the day of her accident, back at her flat. They had sat chatting and laughing for some considerable time. Mrs Baron had seemed to need company, and Petra had been willing to provide it. It was obvious that, no matter how much the elderly lady might jokingly criticise her son, she was deeply fond of him. After one good laugh, she had actually said to Petra, 'Oh, why doesn't that son of mine find someone to have a laugh like that with? Laughter has been so lacking in his life in recent months.'

Was it just possible that by staying on in Granville Row she might manage not only to please herself, but also to humanise this man a little for Mrs Baron? Petra had never been the kind of girl to refuse a challenge, and, as challenges went, this was a big one. She would give herself the lunch-hour to see what this man was really like and to weigh up all her options.

He took Petra to a smart restaurant in one of the town's Georgian terraces. A parking place and a table appeared as though to order, and it was obvious from the waiter's greeting that Hugo Baron was no new customer.

He gave Petra's Edwardian leg-of-mutton-sleeved cambric blouse a thoughtful look as she took off her cloak.

'Yes, you're right,' she said, getting in her comment before his. 'Another genuine antique, and I love it.'

'I don't deny its attractiveness. But do you never feel a leaning towards contemporary fashion?'

'The skirt's modern enough, though Laura Ashley—
if the name means anything to you—does rather go for
a period look. The pin-tucks match those on the blouse,
see? But if you mean am I turned on by such things as
the mini's renaissance, the answer's not really. I know
what I like, and what I like tends to be the old and even
the demure.'

He gave her a quizzical look. 'I imagine you can
counterbalance the demure effect without too much
trouble.'

At that point the waiter brought over menus, and the
business of selecting lunch took over. Both opted for the
self-service hors-d'oeuvres, followed by medallions of
beef with onion and chestnut sauce for Hugo Baron and
monkfish in filo pastry with mussel, wine and shallot
sauce for Petra.

When they were seated again after their trip to the
hors-d'oeuvres table, he began to question Petra about
her involvement in the antiques market.

'I got into it by accident, really,' she told him. 'I had
an aunt from whom I inherited the contents of a house
in which generations of people had never thrown a thing
away, it seemed. I did an experimental boot fair, selling
a surprising amount, and moreover I enjoyed the experience. From there it snowballed.'

He was frowning. 'But it's not exactly a career, is it?
How old are you?'

'Not old enough to mind being asked—or young
enough to resent it, either! I'm twenty-three.'

'And how long have you been dabbling in antiques?'

'About eighteen months.'

'So you must have done something else first?'

'I didn't have another serious job, if that's what you
mean.'

'College, then? University?'

'I'm flattered by the assumption, but no.'

He digested this in silence for a moment, the frown now seeming permanently established. 'You must have done something in the three years—at the most conservative estimate—between school and the start of your business venture.'

She was enjoying teasing his curiosity. 'I kept busy doing this and that.'

'This and that? With the work market in the dodgy state it's been in for heaven knows how long?'

She led him a little further along the disapproving path.

'I helped in a shop. Delivered papers on occasions. Did the odd bit of cleaning and the odd bit of home-help work.' All of which had strong family connections, but of the major purpose behind all her various activities she was saying nothing as yet. Her aim in life had been blazingly clear during those years, and it was nobody's business but hers.

'It hardly sounds like a career.'

'I wasn't exactly thinking in terms of a career at the time,' she answered.

'But you had to live. That calls for money, and a career structure of some kind is generally considered to be what leads to it.'

'I got by.'

The main course arrived just as Petra was beginning to tire of the interrogation. She made a determined attempt to divert the conversation into more general channels, but Hugo Baron was a very persistent man and he returned eventually to the puzzling question—to him—of her past, present and future.

'I find it difficult to understand how anyone can drift through life as you have apparently done. Do you never worry about making ends meet? You're not in a very lucrative business. You haven't even managed to get settled premises as yet.'

Petra decided it was time to relent slightly. 'I'm not quite as butterfly-brained as you think. The aunt who left me the contents of her home also left me the house itself. I had it divided into three flats. I have the ground-floor one, and I rent out the other two. Manda and Joe—you met them briefly—have the first floor, and a school-teacher has the top flat. All of which provides me with regular income, and affords me the freedom to do a little of what I like.'

Even this did not satisfy him. He leaned towards her, still spurred by exasperation. 'But what about the overall *plan* for your life?'

Petra smiled sweetly. 'I don't have one. Life's too short to be docketed and arranged and fitted into pigeon holes. Put me down as the prime Miss World type, who just wants to "enjoy life, travel and meet people".'

He sat back. 'You've got a little more between your ears than the average beauty-contest candidate.' The green eyes scanned her face. 'Though you're pretty enough. I grant you that.'

Petra did not give him the satisfaction of a reply to that. Compliment it might have been, but to her it smacked of the patronising. She had enjoyed leading the stuffed shirt on with a rather distorted view of her life up to date, but now it was time that the game ended.

'Leaving aside our differing attitudes towards life,' she said, 'that was an absolutely delicious meal.'

'Would you like a dessert?'

'Just coffee, thanks. Not a crumb more.'

He sorted out the coffee question with quiet authority. Petra sipped hers, then said, 'I'd like you to stop by and have a look at Collections before we have our final discussion.'

He looked at her. 'I can't really see the need for that.'

'You've condemned my business without seeing how I intend running it. Is that fair?'

'A pretty arrangement of goods isn't going to change the basic situation.'

She faced him with determination. 'Nevertheless, I have gone along with your suggestion that I should look at other premises. Now I'm asking you to fall in with a suggestion of mine.'

He shrugged. 'Have it your way, then. Though I can't promise it will have the remotest effect on my thought processes.'

The remotest effect on his thought processes! How pompous could you get? He might think she looked like something out of Jane Austen, but he was the one who sounded like a Darcy or a Knightley.

Back at Granville Row she went ahead of him into the shop. He followed her, just far enough behind to cause the indiscretion but close enough to hear Manda's, 'At last! I was beginning to think he'd eaten you!'

'No. I decided against dessert,' Hugo Baron said, straight-faced.

'Oh, gosh! That's my cue to exit up-stage right again,' Manda said, heading for the kitchen.

There were no customers, and he was able to walk round in peace. Petra stood waiting for the inspection to be completed.

'Well?' she enquired briefly when he eventually walked back to join her at the door.

'Do you know that the drum table on which you've displayed that motley collection of tongs is worth the rest of your stock put together—and more?' he said.

Petra felt a surge of annoyance. 'Well, it's not for sale. Nor is it what you're supposed to be concentrating on.'

He stared down at her, making her wait a moment longer.

'I suppose you've done very well with the resources available to you,' he said eventually, in a patronising tone calculated to set Petra's hackles rising.

Oh, brother! Do you need taking down a peg or two! she thought. With hypocritical demureness she lowered her eyes and said, 'Why, thank you, Mr Baron.'

Once in his office again, she wasted no time in getting down to the business of telling him what she had decided.

'I have one question to ask,' she began. 'Am I right in thinking that my lease is watertight if I want to hold on to it?'

'You are.' His mouth set in a firm, disapproving line, but at least he made no attempt to pretend otherwise.

'Then let me tell you my thoughts after seeing the Mortimer Street shop. The premises are good, and were I not in the position of having to compare them with Granville Row I would probably jump at them. But the position of that shop doesn't compare at all favourably with Granville Row. Banks, building societies and businesses all around. Very little in the way of passing potential clients, I imagine. Just a trickle of workers intent on getting to work, bank the profits, and go home— whereas in Granville Row I'm likely to attract passing interest from people going to the hairdresser's, the beauty salon, the bookshop, the delicatessen . . . not to mention the fact that we are set back from a main road with our own parking. Who knows, Mr Baron? Even your own clients may well be tempted to slum it in Collections.' She looked him squarely in the face, prepared for his reaction. 'This chance came out of the blue for me. I didn't seek it, and I didn't dream of it. But it was offered to me, and I was always encouraged to take everything life offers and make the most of it. So I'm sorry to disappoint you—but I prefer to stay put in Granville Row. It won't be for long, after all, and I hope we can both be civilised about it.'

Her heartbeat speeded up while he kept her waiting for his reply. When it came, however, it was not what she was expecting.

'You said you weren't butterfly-brained,' he said reflectively, 'and I think you've just proved it. That's a very shrewd summing-up of the choices offered to you, Miss Collins.' He pressed a buzzer on his desk without more ado, and the girl in the outer office came in at once. 'Let Miss Collins have a copy of the Granville Row terms and conditions when she leaves in a moment, will you, Laura?' he said.

Petra felt rather deflated. She had keyed herself up for a full-scale battle, and been offered hardly the smallest skirmish.

'Thank you for taking it like this,' she said, standing.

He rose and looked down at her, and there was more grey than green in his eyes, causing her suddenly to think again.

'I'm a civilised man, Miss Collins. I have stated my position and you have stated yours. The situation is there, and we shall no doubt manage to live with it. You will not find me sending in the heavies to get rid of you. But make no mistake, I shall be watching every move you make. You will be in Granville Row, but on my terms. And you will get away with nothing, believe me. Please pick up the papers I mentioned on the way out.'

She hesitated. 'In the circumstances, perhaps you would at least agree to my paying for my own lunch?'

Now he gave her a look of incredible fury. 'For heaven's sake! Lunch was of no importance whatsoever.'

Petra left with as much dignity as she could muster, and drove back to the shop, where Manda was agog to hear all that had happened.

It was only just after nine on Monday morning when Petra had her next encounter with Hugo Baron.

It was a glorious Indian-summer day. Petra had put on a pretty, full-skirted "New Look" dress from the forties—a happy Camden Market find—and she had wedged the shop door invitingly open, putting two willow-pattern umbrella stands holding walking sticks with elaborately carved heads on each side of the doorway on the pavement to lure people inside.

Hugo Baron was the first person through the door. Petra, in love with the whole human race on a day like this, gave him a beaming smile.

'Good morning! Isn't it glorious?'

He gestured towards her doorway display. 'No goods are to be displayed on the shop frontage. Clause 3a states that quite clearly.'

Petra's smile faded. 'I'm sorry. I didn't know, and they hardly take up any space, so I didn't think they would be an obstruction. I'll bring them in.'

'If you had taken the trouble to read the papers you took home from my office on Saturday, you would have known that.'

'I had a very busy weekend.' In fact, she had completely forgotten them. She made to go past him to bring in the heavy umbrella stands.

'Allow me.' He picked up one in each hand as though they were no bigger than milk bottles. 'Where would you like them put?'

'Anywhere, thank you,' Petra said stiffly.

He took her at her word. At the shop door he turned. 'As you observed, a glorious day. Good morning.'

There had been a hint of satisfaction in his eyes, though he had not allowed a flicker of it to reach his inscrutable features.

Petra felt that some of the sparkle had been rubbed off the day. She went over to her bag and fished out the terms and conditions, which were where she had put them on leaving the Baron Estates office two days ago. She had better get genned up on what was on, and what wasn't on in Granville Row. She might have got herself an amazingly cheap lease for the next three months, but all the signs indicated that it wasn't going to be an easy one.

As for softening up the stuffed shirt—she might as well forget all about that crazy idea. She doubted that anyone could do it.

# CHAPTER THREE

IT HAD been one of those grey, drizzling days that made all but the most hardened shopper stay at home. It was only now, twenty minutes before closing time, that the rain had stopped and the pavements dried, but far too late to bring any benefit to shopkeepers.

Petra had seen the small boy hanging around on and off for the past quarter of an hour, obviously fascinated by the display of old mechanical toys in the Collections window.

He was a nice-looking child, wearing the grey and scarlet uniform of the nearby junior school, and around seven or eight years old. He had the appealing, over-large front teeth of his age-group, yet to be grown into. He had taken off his cap, revealing dark, glossy hair with a tuft that stood up on the crown of his head. His eyes were solemn and dark, and his chin determined though still childishly rounded, and, in common with all boys of his age that Petra had encountered, his shirt-tail had escaped his shorts and hung down below his blazer at the back.

At a loose end herself, and just waiting for closing time, she went over to the window and wound up the monkey with the drum, then set him down to perform, smiling at the boy through the glass. He gave her a quick, delighted grin, and watched the monkey until it stopped.

Petra went to the door.

'Are you waiting for someone?' she asked, thinking his mother was perhaps having her hair done further along the Row.

'I have to wait every day,' he said resignedly.

So it couldn't be a hair-do, unless he had the most self-indulgent mother in the world. Perhaps she worked in one of the Granville Row shops, which meant that the poor kid had to hang around between four and five-thirty from Monday to Friday.

'I haven't seen you before,' she said.

'That's because it's been half-term. I've been staying with my grandmother.'

'I bet she spoils you.'

The wide grin appeared again. 'She lets me have sweets every day.'

'Sounds the right sort of grandma to me. Do you want to see the rest of these things working? You can come inside if you like—if it's all right for you to do that,' she added.

'I'm allowed to go to the end of the shops both ways.'

'That's all right, then.'

He followed her into the shop and watched while she wound up the two dogs on a see-saw. When the see-saw had ground to a halt he looked around.

'This used to be dresses and things.'

'And now it's me and my bits and pieces.'

'Better than old dresses.'

Petra smiled at him. 'What's your name, then?'

'Alexander.'

'And mine's Petra. So now we're introduced.' They worked through the mechanical toys, then Alexander's attention turned to the glass jar of marbles.

'Do you play?' Petra asked, picking a handful out.

'Yes. But these are different from mine.'

'That's because they're old.'

'I didn't know there were old marbles. This is a funny one.' He picked out the Chinaman, turning it over in ink-stained fingers.

'It's much heavier than the rest. Have a go. Try aiming at this one.' She rolled a cat's eye down the shop. Alexander sent the Chinaman after it, but the thick-pile carpet affected the speed of both.

'Not much good in here,' Petra said. 'Come and try it outside, only not near the drain. I've nearly lost it down there before.'

It was quiet and the lay-by was empty. The pair of them squatted down on the washed-clean ground and embarked on a serious game with five marbles each. The score had swung to Alexander eight, Petra two, when a voice caused both of them to look round guiltily.

'Not the most appropriate place for playing marbles,' Hugo Baron said.

Petra scrambled guiltily to her feet and Alexander edged towards the pavement. Hugo Baron was looking at the boy, who suddenly seemed a very little boy indeed at the side of this huge man.

'You've taken up enough of Miss Collins's time, Alexander. You'd better go and wash those grubby hands before we go home,' he said.

*We* go home? Petra's mental image of the man suddenly had to undergo an incredulous rethink. So far it had been trouble enough just thinking of him in his professional relationship to herself. Now she was forced to widen the canvas, link him with someone else. Was he minder, uncle or—most unbelievably of all—father to Alexander? Father! That was certainly a difficult one to cope with. It was difficult to believe that he could ever have permitted himself to be so undisciplined as to love someone and actually father a child.

Alexander proved that it was so. 'Petra's been showing me all her toys, Dad,' he said.

'Then you must thank *Miss Collins*.' The emphasis on the name was not lost on the boy.

'She told me to call her Petra.'

'But Miss Collins would be more polite.' This time the dark eyebrows drew closer together, reinforcing the meaning.

'Thank you, Miss Collins,' Alexander said, subdued, giving back the marbles.

'Keep this one to bowl them over at school,' Petra told him, dropping the Chinaman into his hand.

The beaming smile flashed out. 'Oh—great! Thanks, Pe—Miss Collins.' He ran off into the antiques shop before his father could intervene, stuffing the Chinaman into his pocket.

'I thought that you only had one Chinaman,' Hugo Baron said, and she couldn't tell whether he was mocking or reproving her.

'So I have—but it will have much more glory with Alexander.' She looked up at him. 'Fancy you having a son.'

'It's quite a common state of affairs for a man to have a son. And to be concerned when he sees him being encouraged to play marbles in the road,' he added pointedly.

Petra misunderstood.

'Was I lowering the tone of Granville Row again? Sorry—but you can't claim that there's anything about marbles in the terms and conditions, because I *have* read them from beginning to end now. You have a very nice little boy. I was enjoying spending time with him.'

He looked at her with pitying scorn. 'If you ever grow up enough to have a child of your own, Miss Collins, you will perhaps realise that a parent spends a lot of time instilling road-safety precautions into a child. Playing in the possible path of cars isn't exactly recommended behaviour. I too think Alexander is a nice little boy. I'd like him to have the chance of growing up.'

Petra went on the defensive. 'There was no traffic around. You can see that for yourself.'

'But there could be. It's the principle that counts.'

She was well and truly in the wrong, and she knew it. But something about this man brought out all her fighting spirit.

'Like the principle that had you doing your damnedest to keep me out of Granville Row?' she asked.

'Now you're confusing two separate and entirely different issues. Though, now you mention it, it does happen to be the first time I've seen any tenants of Granville Row squatting in the gutter to play marbles. Tell me . . .' His eyes took in every detail of what she was wearing today, actually the national costume of a minor European country, a very pretty bargain she had picked up in an ethnic textile dealer's in London, but obviously giving a different impression to him. 'Is that a gypsy's outfit you're wearing?' The link between the question and his previous statement about her behaviour didn't need reinforcing. He turned towards his shop, not waiting for an answer.

'Pompous ass!' Petra said under her breath, but not quite low enough for him not to hear.

'I think the ability to admit oneself in the wrong without growing abusive is very worthy, don't you?' he said, and disappeared into Granville Antiques.

Petra flounced into her own premises and slammed the door behind her, causing a witchball to come adrift and shatter on the floor. Since she had only left the witchballs in the window to prove to Hugo Baron that she couldn't care less about being suspected of an interest in witchcraft, she was doubly punished. She set about picking up the pieces, wishing that she could grind them up and serve them to the man in his dinner that night.

'So he's actually human enough to have a son, impossible though that seems,' she concluded her account of the afternoon's incident to Manda back at the house that evening.

'Oh, yes. I knew he had,' Manda said surprisingly.

'You knew? How did you know?'

'Margaret Bannister told me.' Margaret was the top-floor tenant in Petra's house. 'I bumped into her the afternoon you had lunch with him and I made that gaffe about thinking he'd eaten you. I told Margaret about it for a laugh, and she said his son was in her class. I forgot all about it afterwards.'

'I wish you'd told me. I need all the advance information I can get about that man.'

Manda raised her eyebrows. 'That particular day, I seem to remember your saying that nothing would please you more than never having to hear of or speak to the man again.'

Petra was brooding on what the schoolteacher had said.

'Did she tell you any more about him?'

'She said he was a nice kid.'

'Not Alexander. His father.'

'She did, as a matter of fact. She said he was a good parent—always there at school functions, generous when it came to donating to funds.'

Petra twisted a strand of hair round her finger thoughtfully.

'And what about Alexander's mother?' It was still strange to think of Hugo Baron with a wife and child.

'She died before the boy started school, apparently, so Margaret never knew her.'

'Oh... if only I'd known!' Petra said, crestfallen.

Manda looked doubtful. 'I can't see what difference it would make. He doesn't strike me as the kind of man to want to discuss private matters with close friends, let alone——' She stopped.

'Let alone with people he can't stand the sight of,' Petra concluded for her. 'Of course he wouldn't want to talk about it, and neither would I. But it would have changed the way I reacted this afternoon if I'd known. It certainly explains his over-protective attitude towards Alexander. I just took it as one more instance of unpleasantness to me.'

'Well, it probably was,' Manda said matter-of-factly.

'Oh, well... It's just one more thing for him to chalk up against me,' Petra said gloomily. 'I unbalance his mother's mind, I insist on dragging his posh shops into the gutter, and now I've had a shot at pushing his son under the passing traffic.'

'Oh, for goodness' sake!' Manda said, yawning. 'Go and cook your dinner. I think your brain's suffering from calorie deprivation.'

Petra found herself looking at Hugo Baron with new eyes, though usually from behind the safe screen of the Collections window. She saw him walk past late one afternoon with Alexander, actually laughing down at the boy, and there was a warmth and affection that transformed the carved granite of his features into something human and alive. Never when he encountered her, though. His words might be conventionally polite, but always there was the barrier at the back of the grey-green eyes, the imperceptible—but not to her—tightening of the jaw.

The idea that Petra had once had of attempting a softening-up process on him to please his mother now seemed ridiculous. Someone might be capable of bringing him back to life again, but not in a million years would it be her.

It was the middle of the following week before Petra saw Alexander to do more than say a brief 'hello' to him. He came into Collections after school one day and stood at the door looking around with a purposeful air.

'Hello.' Petra went over to him. 'How's the Chinaman doing?'

He brought it proudly out of his pocket—a pocket that bulged with more marbles than were good for it. 'It's doing brilliantly. I was afraid to use it at first because I didn't want Nigel Forest to win it. So I practised until I was used to it, and now I can beat Nigel Forest any day.'

'You can always count on a Chinaman,' Petra said gravely. She glanced out of the window, on her guard. 'Does your father know where you are?'

'Yes. I told him I was coming. I want to buy something.'

Petra looked at him with exaggerated respect. 'A customer? What can I do for you, then, sir?'

'You know my grandmother?'

'A little.'

'Well, it's her birthday soon. I thought——' His brows drew together in a frown of concentration, a frown reminiscent of the one so frequently on his father's brow. 'I thought, well, she's old, and old people like old things, so maybe she'd like something from here.'

Petra suppressed a smile at the thought of Mrs Baron's reaction to that candid description of her. 'And what price-range did you have in mind? In other words, how much have you got?'

He fished in the other pocket and brought out an assorted handful of coins. 'Two pounds forty-five pence. I've been saving up.'

Petra knew that there was precious little on display to meet that limited requirement, and all of it honestly labelled with clear prices. But she had a newly acquired box of oddments from a house sale she had attended at the weekend, not really looked at properly, and certainly not priced.

'Why don't you have a look through this?' she said, opening the door to get the box off the stairs. 'New stock that no one has seen yet, so you might find yourself a bargain. Nothing over three pounds in there, I think.'

She left him happily ferreting through the box and dealt with a couple of customers. When the second customer left, Alexander was waiting with an oblong, dark metal box in his hand and a look of pleasure on his face.

'I think Grandma would like the pattern on this,' he said. 'It's dirty, but it might clean up, do you think?'

'Where did you find it?' Petra asked after a brief hesitation.

'In the bottom of that broken wooden box. The bottom lifts up, and this box was under there.'

The wooden box, intended to hold cigarettes, must have been meant to contain musical works in its base. Now it just held the crumpled paper which must have packed Alexander's find securely so that no betraying rattle had warned of its presence when she had first looked through the job lot of items.

'Don't you think it will clean up?' he asked doubtfully, misinterpreting her silence.

'Oh, I'm sure it will,' Petra said, handing it back to him. It should. It was solid silver, and old. She looked at Alexander's face. 'Well, Alexander,' she said, 'I think this will be a lovely surprise for your grandma.' That was the understatement of the year, but if anyone deserved an unexpected bargain from Collections Mrs Baron did. It had only been surprise that made Petra hesitate, not the least shadow of doubt that what she had said to the child must stand.

'I've got enough?' He was fumbling out his five, ten, and fifty-pence coins.

'Just. But I'm afraid it's going to take all you've got.'

'That's all right. I didn't want anything cheap,' he said grandly.

Petra wrapped the box in tissue paper, gave him some advice on cleaning it, and sent him proudly on his way with his purchase.

She should have known that that wouldn't be the end of it. Not much more than five minutes later, the phone rang.

'Baron here,' an unmistakable voice said.

'Oh, yes. Good afternoon, Mr Baron,' Petra said, mentally girding her loins for battle. 'How are you?'

'Surprised, to say the least of it,' he replied without further delay. 'Do you realise what you've done?'

'I know perfectly well what I've done, and I stand by it,' she said calmly, but with unmistakable firmness.

'You have sold an eighteenth-century patch-box of some considerable value for a few pence.'

'I have sold an item from my fixed-price box at the price stated,' she corrected.

There was a brief silence.

'Do you think you are in the right business?' Hugo Baron asked abruptly. 'My seven-year-old son noticed the hallmark on the box. Why on earth didn't you?'

'Mr Baron, I assure you I knew exactly what I was doing. In my book, a bargain is a bargain.'

'In mine, a bad one is something to be avoided at all costs. And certainly something never to be entered into knowingly, if that is what you really are claiming to have done.'

'We're both in the business of finding bargains and selling them at profit. Sometimes the dice lands in the customer's favour. That happened with Alexander. He had the good taste and good luck to pick out the patch-box in a "nothing over three pounds" collection—so congratulations to him.'

'He tells me you didn't know it was there.'

'No. But that makes no difference. That was Alexander's good fortune.'

'To me it smacks more of your charity, and I have no intention of allowing my boy to develop a taste for that. Are you alone?'

'Why?' Petra asked irritably. 'Mr Baron—please let the matter drop. It really isn't anything I want to argue about.'

'I'm coming round.' The phone went dead.

'Oh—damn you and your interfering unpleasantness,' Petra told the innocent phone. Well, he might come marching round, but she wouldn't give an inch. She would show him whether he could dictate her terms of business or not. He might own the premises, but he didn't own her. She stood watching the window, two spots of colour in her cheeks.

The wind was taken completely out of her sails by the fact that when Hugo Baron appeared he was holding a subdued Alexander by the hand. He put the silver box down on the drum table under Petra's nose.

'Alexander and I have had a talk about this,' he began, 'and we are both agreed that it would be quite wrong for him to accept a silver box for the amount he gave you. Isn't that so, Alexander?'

Alexander nodded unenthusiastically. He looked as though the agreement had not been reached without the aid of a few tears.

Petra felt powerless fury welling up inside her. With the child himself here, and looking so downtrodden about the whole business when it should have been so happy for him, how could she make things worse by rowing with his father? But how could she bring herself to give in?

She was saved from an immediate decision by the sight of Mrs Baron passing the window, then stopping and doing a double-take as she realised that her son and grandson were in Collections.

'We can't talk now. Your mother's here,' Petra said hurriedly.

'Don't tell her!' Alexander begged anxiously.

'Of course not.'

Mrs Baron pushed open the door. 'So here you are!' She kissed her son and grandson lightly. 'Hello, both. Ready to come for tea with me, Alexander? I've got cream buns in this bag.' She turned to Petra. 'How nice you've made everything look in here, hasn't she, Hugo?'

Petra had the satisfaction of seeing him forced into expressing muted agreement.

'Mr Baron has taken a very keen interest in everything I've done so far,' she said maliciously, but with the brightest of smiles on her face.

'*Mr Baron*? I thought you young people were all for informality?' Mrs Baron said innocently.

'I find your son's old-world courtesy refreshing,' Petra said. 'You don't encounter that sort of attitude much these days.'

Hugo Baron said nothing, but looked volumes. The silver box in its tissue paper sat on the drum table, metaphorically ticking away like a time bomb.

'So, what does it feel like to be working from your own shop?' Mrs Baron asked Petra brightly.

'I'm finding it an unforgettable experience,' Petra said with absolute sincerity.

Hugo Baron had had enough. 'Let me run you both round to your flat, Mother,' he said abruptly.

'Oh, I think we'll walk, dear,' his mother told him. 'We need to call in at Mitchell's to pay my paper bill, don't we, Alexander?'

From the brightening of Alexander's face, Petra guessed that paying the paper bill was a euphemism for buying sweets. She hoped very much that cream buns and chocolate or whatever would sweeten the sour taste left by the wretched silver box, with which she had by no means finished.

'In that case, let me see you on your way,' Hugo Baron said, hurriedly driving them ahead of him towards the door as if he were the kind of unpredictable farm dog that nipped first and thought later.

Petra contained herself until she had seen Hugo Baron go back into his shop alone and Mrs Baron and Alexander walk off in the direction of Mitchell's further along the road.

She picked up the silver box, locked up her shop, and marched determinedly into Granville Antiques.

'Can I——?' the secretary began, but Petra was already through Hugo Baron's office door, which she closed behind herself with a decisive click.

She went up to his desk and put the box crisply down on it.

'I couldn't speak as freely as I wanted to, a few moments ago, with Alexander there,' she began. 'But I can tell you now that I found your cowardly hiding behind a seven-year-old to pull off what you wanted to do about as despicable as anything I've seen.'

He looked coolly up into her glowing face. 'You appear to be speaking freely enough now,' he said drily.

'And I have by no means finished. I haven't the least intention of going back on my word to a child, and I'm surprised that even you could wish me to do so. Don't you realise how badly you've disappointed Alexander by what you did just now? Don't you know how you've hurt him?'

'Life hurts,' Hugo Baron said shortly. 'Nobody's immune from learning that.'

'But at seven years old?' Petra cried passionately. 'What are you? A fish or a reptile or something? Doesn't anything warm flow in your veins?'

'To judge by your over-emotional language, you've got enough warmth, albeit of a suspect nature, for both of us. Why don't you sit down and attempt to think rationally about this business?' he invited maddeningly.

'I haven't the least desire to sit, and my thinking's been done already. As far as I'm concerned, your boy made a genuine find in a box of what you would no doubt call trash, and about which I had stated quite firmly that there was nothing in it costing more than three pounds. That's how it was, that's how it is, and I'm not going to do a damned thing to change it.'

'So what exactly are you suggesting that I do?' he asked with dangerous calm.

'Just let the situation stand. Let Alexander have his present for his grandmother.'

'But Alexander knows that the present is worth many times what he paid for it.'

'Only because you told him that. Tell him . . . tell him that you made a mistake, that your estimate was wrong— that someone who knows better has valued it at a very low price.'

'So—just let me recap,' he said, a reasonable note in his voice that managed at the same time to sound menacing. 'You want me to deceive my son on what his pocket money is capable of buying, and, in order to achieve this deception, you suggest that I lie to him.'

'That's just words. You can make words have any emphasis you like if you're crafty enough,' Petra said hotly.

'It seems a pretty fair summing-up of your recommendation. I'm afraid it isn't one I can go along with.'

'Then I'll leave you to deal with the damned box as you think fit. As far as I'm concerned, it has an aura as black as night around it, and I don't want to set eyes on it again. I'm certainly not taking it back. Nor am I refunding Alexander's money. You can do that yourself. And you can throw the box in the river for all I care.'

He looked at her with cold self-control. 'You're not the first person I've known with an irrational line of argument and an extreme reaction to not getting her own way.'

'Possibly I'm not,' Petra rapped back at him. 'Whoever the other one was, she has my heartfelt sympathy. She must have felt she was talking to the north face of the Eiger.'

She turned on her heel, a seething mass of frustration, and blazed out of the shop. It was only five-fifteen, but she was going home right away. If she had to encounter Hugo Baron once more this afternoon, she couldn't answer for what she might do. Throw the contents of her shop at him, most likely—and that wouldn't do her the least bit of good.

All next day she was on guard, expecting further communication from next door, but the silence of the grave floated her way from Granville Antiques.

By closing time she had begun to think that, miserable though it was from Alexander's point of view, the matter was closed. But no sooner had she allowed herself to think that than the shop door opened and Hugo Baron and Alexander came in. Hugo Baron turned the shop door sign to 'Closed', then they approached Petra.

'Alexander has something to tell you,' he said calmly.

'Another case of the human shield? Say on, then, Alexander.'

The child was obviously bursting to say his piece. 'We've sold the box. Dad said you told him to do something like that. You'll never guess how much we got for it!'

Petra was speechless for a second. 'I don't suppose I shall,' she managed to say eventually. 'But, as your father said, I left it up to him.' She looked pure contempt at Hugo Baron. 'I'm sure I shall be expected to congratulate you on a smart deal.'

'One hundred and seventy-five pounds!' Alexander said triumphantly.

Petra felt sick. Not because of the amount, but because of the lesson in materialism that Alexander was being taught.

'I expect your father is glad for you to have that kind of business experience,' she couldn't stop herself saying.

'Tell Miss Collins what we've decided,' Hugo Baron said calmly.

Alexander warmed to his subject. 'My dad says that because I was the one who spotted the box I should make a good profit, so he's giving me enough to buy some of Grandma's favourite perfume. So that's all right.' His face lost its excited glow slightly. 'Well ... not quite as all right as giving her the box, but still ...' His voice tailed off, then he brightened up again. 'Still, that wouldn't have been fair.'

Petra's eyes stared unrelentingly into Hugo Baron's, conveying, she hoped, exactly what she was thinking. 'So now both you and your father will make a profit. That's much more fair, isn't it?'

'Oh, no!' Alexander's voice was shocked. Hugo Baron watched Petra steadily, a slight, infuriating smile playing round the corner of his mouth. 'You tell her the rest, Dad,' Alexander said urgently, tugging at his father's hand.

'Very well.' He smiled at his son, then the grey-green eyes looked directly into Petra's again. 'Alexander and I thought that the rest of the money should really be divided between us—half to you, because the box was yours though you made it clear that you didn't want to profit from it, and half to me for recognising its worth and insisting on doing something about it. But I know that trying to effect that arrangement would mean trouble, so we wondered if you would agree to having a meal with me at Quaglino's, say? That would remove the need to go into any further division of profits.'

Before Petra had the chance to reply, the shop door was opened and Hugo Baron's secretary burst in breathlessly.

'I'm sorry to interrupt, Mr Baron, but the auction rooms are on the phone. They have to speak to you urgently. They've got a transatlantic caller on a line to them.'

He detached himself from his son's hand. 'Excuse me a moment. I'll be back. Wait here, Alexander.' He followed his secretary hastily out of the shop.

Alexander looked eagerly at Petra. 'You will, won't you? Go to Quaglino's with my dad, I mean?'

Petra knew Quaglino's, but only by reputation. As far as its prices were concerned, you might as well eat solid and drink liquid gold—that was the generally held opinion. Certainly an eating experience to remember, if your bank balance could stand the strain. And certainly calculated to do away with any profits from the wretched box.

She looked at the child's face, and he looked back at her, wide-eyed hope unaccountably written all over him.

'It really isn't necessary, Alexander,' she said lamely.

'But I want you to!'

'Why is it so important?'

'Because—because my dad never does anything like that any more.'

'Perhaps he doesn't want to. Perhaps he's happier doing other things.' Like beating up old ladies and torturing babies and spoiling his own son's pleasure, she thought savagely.

'But now he's decided to do this. If you don't go, he'll be back to stodging. That's what Grandma calls it. She says it would do him good to get revolved with someone who likes a bit of fun.'

Hugo Baron had come silently back into the shop. '*Involved*,' he said grimly. 'And when you are a little older, Alexander, you will learn that there are certain remarks of your grandmother's that it is politic to repeat, and certain others that it is wiser to forget at once.' He looked at Petra. 'Well—tell me, have we got this business settled?'

Petra was aware of Alexander doing a little up-and-down jig in suppressed excitement. She weighed up the pros and cons of the situation. Con—she hadn't the least desire to go anywhere with this unsufferable man. Pro— if she refused, she would disappoint a nice little boy. Moreover, if the solution to the problem of the wretched box did not include her, it seemed quite likely that Alexander would develop a guilt complex about the perfume he could now afford for his grandmother.

'I suppose so,' she said ungraciously.

Alexander gave a little cheer, and was promptly told that that would do, and ordered to go back to the shop and get ready for home. 'I'll be with you in a moment,' his father concluded.

When they were alone in Collections, he said stiffly to Petra, 'Thank you for agreeing to my suggestion. Alexander set great store by it. He has a strong sense of fair play.'

Petra could now let her suppressed resentment at being manipulated rip. 'I'd like you to know that in normal circumstances I'd rather jump in a vat of hot oil than agree to spend time in your company,' she said with feeling. 'The only reason I've agreed is to allow that unaccountably nice son of yours to forget he ever contemplated giving his grandmother a tarnished old box for her birthday.'

'Whatever the reason, the thanks still stand,' he said smoothly.

'And I haven't, by the way, agreed to a meal at a showy restaurant. Quite frankly, it would make me sick. I'll have one drink in any pub you care to go to for the sake of Alexander thinking we've divided the spoils, then that's it.'

'We'll settle that at the time.' He scanned her hot, furious face, then allowed himself a small smile. 'So, Irish, what about fixing a date?'

'The sooner the better. Let's get it over,' Petra said curtly.

'Saturday, then, if you really can't bear to wait?'

She turned a look of unadulterated venom on him. 'Saturday is as good as any day. I know these premises are yours, but I'd advise you to leave them right now.'

'I had it in mind to do just that, since Alexander is waiting. Until Saturday, then.' He nodded briefly and departed.


'What's got into you?' Manda asked, reading Petra's face that evening.

Petra told her.

'The chance of a free meal at Quaglino's, and you look like that? You must be crazier than I thought.'

'But in the company of a creep like him! Believe me, Manda, if you'd had the encounters with the man that I have, you'd realise it won't exactly be a picnic.'

Manda sat back, eyes narrowed thoughtfully, hugging her coffee-mug as she looked at Petra. 'I think there's more to this Hugo than meets the eye. For someone who doesn't want you around, he's certainly going out of his way to see enough of you.'

Petra gave a scornful laugh. 'Rubbish. It's all his idea of the right thing and fair play and showing a gypsy like me how the correct set do things.' She made an effort to shrug the subject away. 'How about another cup of coffee? And weren't you going to show me the wedding dress you're working on?'

'Now you're changing the subject,' Manda said, eyes dancing. 'Always very revealing when a girl does that.'

'Manda!' Petra threatened.

Manda grinned. 'OK. The wedding dress. Come through and have a look at it.' She gave Petra a cheeky grin over her shoulder. 'Some people, of course, would see a Freudian link between talk of Hugo Baron turning to talk of wedding dresses.'

'And it would be the last link they invented before the men in white coats turned up to take them away,' Petra said with feeling. 'Just drop it, Manda, will you?'

Manda heard the note in Petra's voice, and dropped it.

# CHAPTER FOUR

PETRA had given considerable thought to what she should wear on Saturday evening, but not for the usual reasons influencing a girl on her first outing with a man.

She heard the car draw up in front of the house and had time for a last quick look at herself before the bell rang. A simple white silk T-shirt tucked into blue jeans. Nothing over-the-top—just adequate to remind Hugo Baron that she was going to a pub, not a showcase of a restaurant. The bell rang. Petra opened the door.

'Good evening,' he said. He was wearing a light grey suit of perfect cut, a snowy white shirt and a silk tie of subtle but arty and modern colour and pattern. He looked quite different from the dark-suited, sober-tied man of the working week. He was also wearing, she saw, a fleeting, puzzled expression, which he quickly schooled into one of enquiry. 'I hope I'm not too early?' he added, avoiding—much too carefully—any tendency of his eyes to look in the direction of her jeans-clad legs.

'Not at all. Bang on time,' Petra told him with a smile. She picked up her wrap—a big shawl with flowers in jewel colours against a black background. 'And I'm quite ready.'

He seemed to have recovered from the initial surprise of her appearance. 'Let's go, then, shall we?'

As they settled in the car, though, she caught him glancing at her legs.

'Is anything wrong?' she asked brightly.

'No. Why should there be? I was merely thinking that this was the first time I'd seen you in anything approaching contemporary dress.' He switched on the engine.

'How is Alexander?' she asked.

'Very well. He asked me to tell you that he hopes you enjoy your meal.'

'You'll have to think up something politic to tell him.' Malicious inspiration struck. 'Tell him that I enjoyed the evening every bit as much as I expected to. No need to say that we went to a pub instead.'

'I should hope not. After all, it's a meal that I invited you to have with me.'

The first stab of unease at his determined tone went through Petra. 'But a drink in a pub was what I accepted.' There was a silence. 'I meant what I said,' she added challengingly.

'Oh, so did I.' He changed gear smoothly and the Alfa Romeo began to eat up and spit out every other car on the road.

Petra gave him a quick glance. His eyes were firmly on the road ahead, but there was the suspicion of a smile she didn't like lurking round the corner of his mouth.

'If you're hungry, I think the King's Arms a little further along does reasonable bar snacks,' she said.

'I don't think we'll trouble to find out.' They passed the King's Arms at the speed of light.

Petra's feeling of unease intensified. 'Are you trying to kill us, by any chance?' she asked him.

He reduced speed. 'Sorry. I didn't realise you were a nervous traveller. I have this ridiculous obsession with getting anywhere on time. No one else bothers, these days, it seems to me.'

'It doesn't exactly matter tonight, does it?'

'I booked a table for eight-thirty. But we'll be there in plenty of time.'

Petra swivelled round in her seat. 'What table?'

'At Quaglino's.'

'Haven't you been listening to me? We're going to have a drink, and that's all.'

He smiled pleasantly. 'I happen to think we're going for a meal.'

'Then you're mistaken,' Petra snapped.

'And I'm driving—so what are you going to do about it?'

The swords were really out now. She reached for the door-handle.

'No good,' he told her. 'Central locking—and I control it.'

It was becoming clearer by the second from the road they were on and the district they were in that Quaglino's was their destination.

'Look, let's not be silly about this,' Petra said persuasively.

'I'm glad you feel like that.'

'We can't possibly go to Quaglino's with me wearing jeans.'

'Not the usual thing, admittedly, but I would never have mentioned it if you hadn't. I thought perhaps you weren't quite *au fait* with the etiquette.'

'I'm wearing them because I'm perfectly "*au fait* with the etiquette",' she said scathingly. 'I haven't the slightest intention of going to Quaglino's,' she added, but unconvincingly, since the car was leaving the road and sweeping up the drive to the restaurant even as she spoke. Petra's face was growing rapidly hotter.

'I don't know what you think you're doing!' she said as the car halted smoothly in a parking space near the door.

'Parking,' he said crisply. He got out and came round to open her door.

She stared straight ahead. 'Don't be so utterly absurd. They'll never let me in.'

'We'll see about that.' He opened the door wider.

'In any case, I refuse to get out. You're not going to make a fool of me.'

'I thought the reverse was the idea,' he said.

One of the restaurant's uniformed minions spoke from the nearby entrance. 'May I do anything for you, Mr Baron?'

'All's well, thanks, George.' He lowered his voice. 'You can either get out of the car under your own steam, or I promise you I shall heave you out like a sack of potatoes and carry you through that doorway myself. Don't doubt for a second that I mean what I say.'

Petra risked a sideways glance at him. He meant it all right. She hesitated. His hand moved towards her. Hurriedly she unfastened the seatbelt and got out.

'Now you're acting like a big girl,' he said, holding her arm in a vice-like grip as he shut the door and operated the locking system.

'Hardly worth doing that!' Petra said scornfully. 'You'll be opening the doors again in seconds.'

'Want to bet? Wait here a moment. And don't dream of bolting. I held the county's fifteen hundred metres record for five years, and I'm still in training.' He went over to the doorman and spoke quietly to him. The doorman disappeared inside, and Hugo Baron imperiously beckoned Petra to approach. 'You can come in now.'

'I can *what*?'

'Come in, as in walk through the door into the restaurant,' he said as though conversing with an idiot.

'Of course I can't,' she said, panicking.

'Then I'll come and give you some assistance.'

Petra hurried up the steps. He held the door open and neatly whisked off her wrap to hand it to the cloakroom attendant. Far from barring the entrance to the restaurant, each member of staff they passed gave them a courteous welcome. Petra even imagined she detected an odd look of sympathy on their faces. She had never in the whole of her twenty-three years felt more conspicuous. She was surrounded by a display of the most fashionable, glamorous and costly dresses Cheltenham's boutiques could produce. In her simple silk shirt and jeans, she felt like a kitchen maid in a debutantes' line-up. If the staff looked strangely and unexpectedly sympathetic, the clientele made up for it. Curious looks and raised eyebrows greeted her passing, and by the time they were shown to one of the most conspicuous tables in the room, on the edge of the dance-floor, Petra would have considered dropping dead a desirable option.

'Couldn't we sit somewhere else?' she asked Hugo Baron desperately.

He looked surprised. 'This is one of the best tables in Quaglino's. How could I possibly ask them to change it?'

She sat down while the waiter fussed over adjusting her chair and handing her the tasselled menu as though she were visiting royalty in a designer dress.

Now that she was seated with only her comparatively suitable top half on view, Petra began to regain her courage. She closed the menu with a snap.

'I ate before we left, but I'm sure you won't let that put you off,' she said.

He surveyed her over the top of his menu. 'If I can threaten to carry you in here, no doubt I can also manage to feed you, but I don't recommend it as desired viewing for our neighbours. Now—it's up to you. You can either choose and eat your own meal, or I will order for you and do whatever else is necessary. I don't believe you had more than soup or cheese, in any case.'

Petra was beginning to realise that she was fighting a losing battle. She might as well give in gracefully, and bide her time. But bide it she would, she promised herself fiercely.

She picked up her menu. 'I'll have melon Lafayette and pheasant royale,' she said. 'The wine's up to you, but I could use a vat of it.'

He smiled. 'Now you're talking. Perhaps we can settle down and enjoy the rest of the evening.'

'And perhaps there really is a Santa Claus!' Petra retorted.

He actually laughed.

She looked assessingly at him. 'You're a different kettle of fish this evening, somehow.'

'Perhaps that's because for once you're not managing to annoy me.'

'Funny, I thought I'd been doing just that.'

'No. You've been providing me with non-stop amusement so far.'

'Nice for you.' She looked at him. 'Tell me one thing. What did you say to the people who run this place to make them let a scruff like me in?'

'I said that there was a reason for your unconventional appearance—which we both know there is. And I asked them how they would feel if they arrived back in this country after working in the Third World, only to find that thieves had ransacked and cleared out the entire contents of their house.'

Petra looked her disgust. 'I thought you were the man who was a stickler for the truth!'

'No untruth was told. I merely didn't elaborate on the reason for the jeans, and I asked them how they would feel about a burglary. The assumption that it had happened to you was theirs.'

'Manipulating words again.' She looked in exasperation at his amused face. 'And they swallowed it.'

'They seemed to. Of course,' he added slowly, looking a little sheepish, 'it also helped somewhat that I happen to own this place.'

The waiter and wine waiter approached to take their orders, giving Petra time to recover from this surprising piece of information.

'You own Quaglino's?' she said when they were alone again.

'I do.'

'And you actually risked knocking its swanky ambience for six by walking in with a girl in jeans?'

'There was a more important issue at the time.'

She shook her head unbelievingly. 'For a man who cares so much about appearances, that was one huge step. Is there more to your empire?'

'A little.'

'No wonder your mother is concerned about your nonstop working.'

'Unnecessarily,' he said dismissively.

'And your son.'

'Alexander? What has he been saying on the subject?'

'A few words on the lines of ''All work and no play'', et cetera. ''Stodging'', he called it.'

'And I know where he got that word from—the fair originator of the stuffed-shirt image.'

'I think they both care about your welfare.'

'I'll grant my mother the honour of being right about one thing. I'm not going to call you Miss Collins all evening. Petra suits the informality of the jeans far better. I offer you ''Hugo'' as a gesture of goodwill.'

'I'll consider it.' For a moment she gave full attention to the melon with its exquisite exotic garnish and sauce. 'Tell me, have you never considered an au pair girl for Alexander? I presume you haven't one at the moment, since he came to the shop after school.'

'No. I decided against it from the start. They never stay long, and I felt he needed a sense of permanence in his life.' A slight shadow seemed to come over his face. 'I realise, of course, that nothing can be wholly permanent.'

'Do you think of marrying again?'

'Never,' he said shortly. 'Tell me, do you have the idea that Christian-name terms means free access to every aspect of someone else's private life?'

'Sorry,' Petra said guiltily, realising that she had been carried away. 'I'm just interested in what makes people tick.'

'Be careful it doesn't lead to tick as in time bomb,' he told her crushingly, but in a second he went on to speak quite lightly of a play he had seen and the dangerous moment passed.

Petra was almost annoyed to find that she was actually enjoying herself. That had certainly not been either scheduled in advance, or augured by the start of the evening. She didn't *want* to enjoy herself. She wanted to let her resentment of being forced into this rarefied atmosphere in her unsuitable clothes fester away until she had the chance to cook up a way of getting her own back. But here she was, true to form, seizing the moment again. Enjoying something it was hard not to enjoy. The food was wonderful. The place, now that the rest of the clientele had forgotten to look down their noses at her, was quite something. And Hugo Baron—Hugo, she thought, trying the name for size and finding that it fitted him extremely well—Hugo was for the moment being far from the stuffed shirt she had grown used to thinking him to be. She glanced at him with resolution. Just you wait, just you wait, though, she thought with relish.

'Food all right?' he asked, catching her fleeting expression.

'Of the gods.' She gave full attention to her pheasant and postponed thoughts of revenge.

He had not quite finished with her, though, she found as she sipped her coffee. A good, discreet group was playing, and several couples were on the dance-floor.

'How about joining them?' Hugo said, his eyes challenging her.

Petra stared at him. 'You're joking.'

'Why should I be?'

'You really mean that I should dance—in *jeans*?'

'Damn the jeans. I'd forgotten all about them.'

'Oh, yes . . . I'll believe that!' she said derisively.

'Believe it or not, it doesn't alter the fact that I feel like dancing. I couldn't care less what you're wearing.'

Petra had that fly-in-a-web feeling again. 'I'm going to the cloakroom,' she said, picking up her bag.

'You won't find a window to escape through.' He was watching her with laughter at the back of his eyes, but she didn't doubt for a moment that he intended to make her go through with his unkind idea.

'If I intended escaping I'd leave by the door,' she told him.

'You won't do that either. The staff have all been warned that you're to be gently persuaded not to leave without me.' His grin broadened. 'Conditions on these Third World assignments can cause a lot of stress, you know. George received that idea with great sympathy, you'll be glad to hear.'

Petra gave him a withering parting look and called on all her courage for the conspicuous walk to the cloakroom. Coming back would be easier, if what she had in mind worked. She was not going to be made even more of a spectacle on the dance-floor if she could help it.

The cloakroom girl hesitated when she asked for her wrap.

'I'm not doing a runner,' Petra said impatiently.

The girl smiled apologetically. 'Sorry, but Mr Baron was concerned about you. It must have been pretty tough out there.'

'No tougher than it is in here,' Petra said with feeling, taking her wrap. She could feel the girl's puzzled eyes on her as she walked over to the cloakroom. No doubt she was putting that odd answer down to the stress of the mythical overseas endeavours.

Petra locked herself in the 'disabled' cubicle, which had a basin and a mirror, and peeled off her jeans. A bit of experimenting resulted in the wrap, which was fortunately as large as her waist was small, becoming a reasonably successful sarong-type skirt. She turned to and fro in front of the mirror. Not bad, but it felt a bit insecure, and she had no pins. Inspiration struck again. There was the black scarf with which she had tied back her hair. She took it off, wrapped it twice round her waist, cummerbund style, and knotted the ends in front. That felt better, and it gave a more finished look.

She ran a comb through her hair and touched up her make-up, and, quite pleased with her improvisation, prepared to face the world again.

'Look after these for me, will you, please?' she said to the attendant as she emerged from her cubicle, airily handing over the jeans. The attendant was too well trained to comment, other than an impassive, 'Certainly, madam.'

At first Hugo didn't appear to realise that the girl approaching the table was the same one who had left it. When the penny dropped, he smiled in acknowledgement and rose to face her as she walked the last few feet towards him.

'What a surprising creature you are!' he said, taking in the details of her transformation.

'I was always encouraged to rise to any challenge,' Petra replied with composure. 'So come on—let's dance.'

He hesitated briefly. 'Can we count on that thing staying in place?'

Petra gave him a mocking glance. 'You mean you're actually scared of attracting attention? In the circumstances, that's rich!'

Dancing with Hugo was a surprising revelation. He was a natural, easy and supple, confounding her expectations yet again. They circled the floor in silence for a while, then he settled her more closely in his arms and said, 'Well, there's always a first, isn't there? This at least is something we're in harmony about.'

'A second, not a first,' Petra said. 'We agree on the merits of Alexander too, don't forget.'

The sequence of slow numbers passed like a dream, and then the group launched into something more vigorous.

'I'm not inclined to tempt providence and put your ingenious transformation at the mercy of this tempo,' Hugo said drily. 'I suggest we have more coffee until they get it out of their systems.'

'Chicken!' Petra said over her shoulder as she led the way back to the table.

He refilled her cup. 'Maybe more caution went into my upbringing than into yours. Who was it who fostered this fighting spirit in you?'

'The same person who told me always to take every opportunity. My father.'

'Tell me about him. He's responsible for rather a lot.'

Dancing had defused the hostility that had marked the earlier part of the evening, and Petra was both fond and proud of her father. She was willing to talk about him.

'Probably the first thing you'd notice about him is that he's paralysed from the waist down,' she said.

He looked sharply at her, his attention fully caught. 'How did that happen?'

'A fall from a horse. He was a jockey—not well-known, but he would have been. The fall happened at a definite upward trend for him.'

'It can't have been easy for him to adjust to the changed circumstances.'

'I'm sure it wasn't. But he regarded it as a challenge to be met. He said nothing could take away all the wild and wonderful things he'd packed into his life up to the accident—so who knew what life might still have in store? Thundering across the turf on a sunny day had been great and he wouldn't have missed a moment of it, but it wasn't everything. There was the rest...' She looked at Hugo, her eyes shining. 'Believe me, when my father told you to seize the moment, you understood only too well what he meant.'

Hugo reached out with unexpected tenderness and touched her hand briefly. 'How old were you when this happened?'

'Just about to leave school.'

'Ah!' he said with understanding. 'So instead of whatever you'd planned, you—what was it? "Did this and that, worked in a shop, delivered papers, did a bit of cleaning and a bit of home-help work"? Now I begin to see the reason for it all.'

'You have amazing recall,' Petra told him.

'For things that surprise me, yes. Now I understand that apparently humdrum recital of activities. How are your parents now? You obviously feel that you can leave them to their own devices at last.'

'My mother queens it over a small empire of Liverpool newsagents, having done her apprenticeship in one to make ends meet after the accident. My father has become a computer buff. He designed a software programme to analyse the performances of racehorses, initially to amuse himself. Now it's in demand world-wide. He does a thousand other things, among which the most important to him is acting as counsellor for an orthopaedic surgeon.'

'That wheelchair must be a pretty high-powered one.'

'Supersonic!'

'And your father sounds to be quite a man.'

'He is.'

He gave her the most genuine smile of the evening. 'And I'm sure he'd say that, with the band playing in more restrained fashion and the dance-floor waiting, the only thing to do is seize the moment and dance.'

She got up readily this time, and going into his arms seemed as natural as breathing. After the tetchiness of the earlier part of the evening, it was good to have called a truce, and to be able to dance in companionable silence. Talking wasn't necessary. The music and the enjoyment of moving in absolute harmony with someone were enough.

Inexplicably, though, when they went back to the table again, the mood had changed, and for the worse. She said lightly, 'I enjoyed that!' and smiled at him as they sat down, and as she spoke she saw the familiar effect of shutters going down at the back of Hugo's eyes. Coming after the brief truce, it was like a blow from a friend. The silence that had been companionable turned into something stressful. Petra couldn't think of anything to say to break it. Expressing enjoyment had apparently been out of order.

Eventually, they spoke together, and on similar lines.

'What time is——?' Petra began.

'I think perhaps it's time to——' Hugo stopped, then shrugged. 'Evidently we're both thinking on the same lines. The girl who is sitting in with Alexander had a twelve o'clock curfew, so I think we'd better call it a day.'

'I thought perhaps your mother would be there.'

'No,' he said crisply. 'My mother needs no encouragement to take a more than healthy interest in my life.'

There was no answer to that. 'I'll go and get my jeans,' Petra said, heading for the cloakroom.

Once in the car, Hugo reached for a soft cashmere travelling rug and told her to put it round her shoulders, but conversation still seemed reluctant to flower again between them. The peace had evidently been a phoney one. But what had turned Hugo back from being pleasant company into the old—yes, the words were sadly appropriate again—the old stuffed shirt?

Petra was the sort of girl who preferred to meet problems head-on, and so just before the end of the journey she said, 'Thank you for the delicious meal. I don't know what I've done to annoy you, but it was unintentional. For a great deal of the evening I admit I was being deliberately confrontational. But not at the end of the evening. Whatever the offence then, it was innocently committed.'

He came to a smooth halt in front of her house and switched off the engine before turning to her.

'You did nothing.' The dim light from the street-lamp fell on her. He was in its shadow, so she felt rather than saw him scanning her face.

'But something happened,' she said.

'Forget it. It's been an unexpectedly pleasant evening. Leave it at that.' He took the rug from her shoulders and tossed it into the back.

'Yes, it has. Though I never thought I should be saying that.'

Her tone forced a shadow of a grin from him. 'You're such an honest creature, aren't you?'

'But you're not,' she said robustly. 'You keep your thoughts knotted away behind that frown, and your feelings tightly buttoned under that old stuffed shirt, don't you?'

'My feelings don't concern you.'

'But their effect jolly well does. And how!'

He sighed in brief exasperation. 'I repeat—you did nothing. If you insist on explanations, this is the only one you're going to get. You simply happen to remind me of someone whose memory is not exactly unadulterated joy.'

'It's hardly fair to let that govern your attitude towards me, is it? Haven't I enough black marks of my own in your book without having someone else's offences attributed to me?' she protested.

'For God's sake, cease fire, Irish!' Before she could reply, he had cupped her chin in his hand and was saying, 'Neither of us exactly suffered too much this evening. Does this convince you?'

It was going to be a light-hearted 'kiss the child better' kiss, she knew that. But it didn't stay that way. From the moment his lips touched hers, the two of them were in the power of something totally unexpected, something that obliterated all trivial thought. A hunger Petra had not known she felt was being satisfied in a way she had never dreamed possible. There was a heady mix of emotions coursing through her, unbidden but all-powerful—fear, triumph, surrender, victory—devastating her with their violence.

And then, as suddenly as the turmoil had been created in her, it was over, and Hugo was drawing away from her, releasing the door-catch with abrupt, indecent haste.

She knew that he had been as affected as she had; his mouth had told her that. But he was quick now to find words to deny it, and his denial cut through the emotions churning inside her with all the pain of a knife.

'So there we are,' he said lightly, and it was only the slight rawness in his voice that told her the truth. 'The traditional end to the evening. The moment seized, in accordance with your philosophy. And, I trust, the debt between us satisfactorily settled.'

Petra would never have believed that such complicated feelings as she had experienced could resolve themselves so rapidly into one concentrated surge of hatred. How dared this odious man so corrupt her father's attitude towards life? How *dared* he?

She got out of the car and looked scathingly down at him.

'The debt settled? If you like. But your pocket was wide open to receive the settlement, Mr Quaglino, which some might consider showed a fair amount of self-interest. As for my philosophy of life, you're light-years away from understanding it. And just one more thing— I like my men to kiss me goodnight because they want to, not because the opportunity's there and they think it traditional. That's one moment that won't be seized again—unless it's over my dead body.' She slammed the car door and stormed towards the house.

Fate, however, was determined not to allow her the upper hand for one compensatory minute. Her angry slamming of the car door had caught in it the edge of her improvised skirt. If she had been moving less violently, no harm would have been done, but the angry force of her progress house-wards tore the precariously fixed fabric from her waist.

Even then, she might have got away unnoticed. Her key was in her hand, and it was very dark.

But fate hadn't finished with her. Someone inside the house, with pitiless timing, switched on the outside light, and there she was, floodlit.

She fumbled the door open, but not before she heard a smothered burst of laughter from the car behind her. In the house, Joe was moving from light-switch to door, the day's empty milk bottles in his hand.

He took in her strangely abbreviated clothing, the slim, bare brown legs, the white lace bikini briefs.

'Must be quite a fella!' he said laconically.

'Shut up!' Petra howled. 'Don't say a word more. All men are lousy bastards!'

Joe grinned, unperturbed, and went out to deposit the bottles while Petra let herself furiously into her own flat.

In the morning she found the folded wrap tucked over her door-handle with a note.

The man swears there's an innocent explanation, but leaves it to you to make it. You've got to come up for lunch and tell all.

Joe, King of the L.B.s.

Petra grinned resignedly, her sense of humour restored, at least as far as Joe and Manda were concerned.

But not *him*. There was no forgiving laughter in her for him.

She ran upstairs to tap on Joe and Manda's door and tell them she'd be up for lunch.

# CHAPTER FIVE

ON MONDAY afternoon Alexander didn't so much come
into Collections as erupt into it.

Petra was dealing with a lady who, after much diligent
sifting through the stock, had at last found two pairs of
tongs to add to her collection—one for asparagus in
silver-gilt, the other dating from the twenties when stylish
flappers held a cigarette in tiny tongs while smoking it.
Over the customer's shoulder, Petra could see an obviously fuming and mutinous Alexander thrashing round
near the door, apparently bursting to unload a grievance.

When the woman had left, Petra went over to the child
and said diplomatically,

'Hello, there. How are you today?'

'I hate him!' Alexander said, grinding a toe into the
carpet then kicking impatiently at the spot in a way that
reminded Petra instantly of Mrs Baron's description of
his father's childhood habit. 'He's the worst man in the
world!'

'Who is?' Petra asked with interest, pretty sure of the
answer and sure too of how much she would sympathise
with it.

'My *father*.' The emphasis on the word put it in the
category of an oath.

'That sounds a bit tough on him.' She couldn't go so
far as to ask what had brought on this attack of fury in
an otherwise nice little boy, but she was certainly
interested to know.

80

'No, it's not tough on him. He's horrid. I don't care if I never go home again.' The dark eyes glistened with threatening tears, belying the words.

'Oh, come on, Alexander!' Petra reproached. 'Home's a pretty good place.'

He looked at her. 'You should have been there on Sunday, then. It was as bad as anything. And it was my grandma's birthday, as well.'

Petra sat down on a little Victorian chair and pushed its twin over to Alexander. 'Why don't you sit down? You're going to dig a hole in that part of the carpet if you go on kicking it like that.'

'Sorry.' He pulled out a school-weary handkerchief and blew his nose. Petra offered him a chocolate caramel which she happened to have in her pocket. The measure of his unhappiness was marked by the fact that he refused it. 'I think it must have been the worst birthday my grandma has ever had,' he said gruffly.

'I expect parts of it were good. Things are never entirely bad,' Petra said encouragingly.

'The food was good—only I was sick afterwards, so even that turned out bad.' His dark eyes looked miserably at Petra, and away again.

'You mean you ate something bad?'

'No. *Did*, not ate. It was all because of that box.'

'Box?'

'Yes. You *know*.'

'The one all the fuss was about? I thought we'd sorted that out. Come on, Alexander. Be reasonable. I'm sure your grandma loved the perfume you gave her.'

'She said she did. Then my father gave her a present— it was a sort of woolly jacket thing; Italian, I think it was. She liked that as well.'

'Sounds all right so far,' Petra commented encouragingly.

'But then my *father*——' again the furious emphasis '—my *father* said there was another surprise, a last-minute one. He took that box—the one I'd wanted to give her and the one he wouldn't let me—out of his pocket. Grandma got excited about it straight away. I knew she would.' His voice wobbled and the big dark eyes stretched wide with outrage.

'Oh, dear,' Petra said quietly, more to herself than the child. She could understand Alexander's outrage at having his gift taken over by someone else—and in particular by the man who had ruined the original intention for it. But, as well as that, she was wondering why on earth she had been made to go through with that farcical meal on Saturday on the proceeds of the sale of a box which, it appeared, had never been sold.

'I felt . . . as though I had something big inside me that was growing and choking me, you know? I didn't mean to spoil her birthday, really I didn't, and I tried hard not to. I didn't say anything. I went out into the garden, but the big thing in me kept on growing and hurting. And then I saw my father's cold frame with his geranium cuttings in it, and there was a rake leaning against it, and I picked up the rake and smashed it down on the glass and broke it in a million pieces. It fell on the cuttings and broke most of them too. And he's stodged away for ages doing them.' His eyes were huge with the memory of his misdeed.

'And what happened then?' Petra asked carefully.

'My father came out and shouted at me, and I shouted back at him. Then Grandma came out and shouted at both of us. She said it was like being in a pit with two fighting dogs, and she was ashamed to think that she had such a horrid son and grandson. After that I was sick. Very. The birthday was ruined. I went to bed, and

Grandma went home all by herself.' He choked on the last word.

'Oh, dear,' Petra said again.

'Alexander!' The voice was deep, male, and very, very angry. Absorbed in Alexander's story as they had both been, neither she nor the little boy had seen Hugo pass the window.

Alexander slipped off his chair, his eyes stubbornly glued to the floor. Petra stood up, but didn't speak.

'You have been told more times than I care to remember that you are to come straight to me when you leave school,' Hugo told the boy grimly. 'Kindly go next door at once and wait for me.'

Alexander gave Petra an imploring, desperate look, then walked warily past his father and out of the shop. When he had gone, Hugo turned on Petra.

'I would be grateful if you would refrain from luring the boy in here every day.'

'I didn't,' Petra told him crisply. 'I was actually busy with a customer when Alexander came in of his own accord. He was obviously upset about something, and I wasn't going to send him away without giving him a sympathetic ear.'

'Which, being roughly interpreted, means that you weren't going to let him go without ferreting around in something that is no business of yours.'

'Any child's unhappiness is the business of whoever happens to come across it and cares sufficiently to do something about it,' Petra retorted swiftly.

'I can deal with my own child's unhappiness perfectly well.'

'Yes. I heard how you did that,' Petra said scathingly, beginning to tick off points on her fingers. 'You took over his present for his grandma, you shouted at him when he didn't like it, and sent him to bed, where he was sick. Full marks for that little venture into child psychology.'

Angry colour suffused Hugo Baron's face, and for a moment Petra thought he was going to strike her, but he attacked her with words, not physical violence.

'Mind your own bloody business!' he snarled. 'It's as much as you can manage to hang on to your clothes.'

'A gentleman wouldn't stoop to a gibe like that,' she told him hotly.

'That shows how much you know about gentlemen,' he said offensively.

'Leaving your pedigree out of it, just don't take your bad temper out on Alexander,' she threatened.

The grey-green eyes, cold as a winter sea, looked down at her. 'What exactly do you think I am? A child-beater?'

'I think you're someone who doesn't fully understand his own child.'

'And you, in your mature wisdom, are dying to explain him to me? I think Alexander and I will manage perfectly well without that doubtful pleasure.'

With a final, sneering look at her skirt, which today was firmly anchored and not about to come adrift and expose her to ridicule, he left, closing the shop door firmly behind him.

Petra served two further customers before closing time, hardly aware of what she was doing, her mind obsessed with the miserable little boy and the angry, uncomprehending man in the shop next door. There was nothing much she could do about it, she told herself. Not now, with Alexander there. Not ever, she concluded ruefully, with a man as sure of his own rectitude as Hugo Baron was.

There was a house sale at a rambling old property on the outskirts of Cheltenham next day. Petra had asked

Manda to stand in for her for the morning at Collections, and was hopeful of building up her stock. She knew via someone involved in the winding up of the estate that the old lady who had just died was the last surviving member of a family of compulsive hoarders. Nothing had been thrown away for several lifetimes, and there were plenty of Petra's type of bits and pieces, she was informed.

What she had not known until she arrived at the house on the day of the sale was that, as well as her kind of thing, the house also was bursting at the seams with items of furniture, some of which were definitely of the quality that Hugo Baron went in for.

She had arrived early to earmark the lot numbers for which she wished to bid, and just before the bidding started she was looking through the contents of an old washbowl in which items not strong enough for individual listing had been gathered together. There were small vases in varying states of repair, some of them quite good, one or two very nice treen, odd metal bits and pieces, and several decorative hatpins of definite interest.

Petra marked off the lot number on her list, and when she looked up her eyes met those of Hugo Baron, who was getting to his feet again after looking thoroughly over a *bonheur-du-jour*.

To her surprise, he came over to her, seemingly prepared to forgive and forget the previous day's heated exchange.

'Good morning,' he said quite pleasantly.

'Good morning.' Petra sought around for something to say. 'Does that interest you?' She nodded at the *bonheur-du-jour*.

'It might, if too many other people aren't equally interested. This is one of your possibles, I take it?' His fingers sifted through the bowl's contents.

'With the same proviso as you made.' She looked over her shoulder. 'I think they're ready for starting.'

'They'll be messing around for a bit longer. Petra——' His hand on her arm detained her as she was about to move away and take her place for the auction.

'Yes?' She looked up into his face.

'I was not exactly on my best form yesterday. I think I owe you an apology. Alexander told me exactly what happened.'

'So did I,' she said defensively.

'I know you did. The trouble is, when Alexander's late, often for no other reason than that small boys are born dawdlers, I find it easy to imagine the worst.'

'But you knew that he was in my shop—and nothing very dreadful is likely to happen to him there.'

'Danger often lurks in the most unexpected places,' he said oddly. He gave her a strange, disconcerting, far-away look, then seemed to snap back into the present. 'In any case, as you pointed out at the time, it was also highly uncivil of me to make reference to an incident you would rather forget.'

'We'll write off that particular episode, I think,' she said decisively.

'Of course—though a bathing costume is every bit as revealing and presumably you wouldn't feel quite so touchy about that.'

'I said forget it,' Petra emphasised.

'And in any case, you have no reason to hide your light, or anything else, under a bushel.' Now she definitely knew that he was deliberately taunting her under the guise of an apology.

'Look, Hugo,' she said impatiently, 'you are either apologising for referring to something a genuinely nice person wouldn't dream of referring to, or you are taking the mickey. I know which alternative I plump for. You don't fool me.'

'It would be a brave man who managed to do that.'

'And as far as I'm concerned,' she said crisply, 'the important fact that emerged yesterday, and which you haven't mentioned so far, is that you are capable of hurting your own son without having the remotest idea why he is hurt. You want to give a bit more attention to that, and less to trying to score points off me.'

That had got under his skin. He was not joking now. 'One thing I do not apologise for is saying that Alexander is my business.'

'Don't worry. I've said all I'm going to say. Excuse me now. I know when I'm addressing a brick wall, and the bidding is going to start.'

She walked off to the other side of the auction-room, wondering why it was that no encounter with Hugo Baron ever progressed to a peaceful conclusion. He was still looking down into the washbowl—heaven knew why—but after a little more ferreting around he came over to lean against the wall on the opposite side of the room as the crowd hushed and the bidding started.

Bidding at an auction was not an occupation that went with a divided mind, and Petra managed to turn her thoughts away from Hugo as the sale progressed. She got the fire-screen she had fancied for a reasonable figure, and several bits of early Derby pottery. Someone else hung on to get the Canterbury she would have liked, but she secured a nursing chair at a lower figure than she anticipated. Hugo, she was aware, snapped up the *bonheur-du-jour*, a set of Hepplewhite library chairs, and a kneehole desk.

The washbowl and its contents didn't come up until towards the end of the list. One other woman seemed keenly interested, then a little way into the bidding a third person joined in.

Petra glanced over to the side of the room from where the bid seemed to have come, and was astonished to see Hugo lowering a hand. She made her own new bid with emphasis, and was rewarded by a formidable frown from Hugo.

The three-cornered battle went on. Petra was growing angrier by the second. What was the man playing at? There was nothing in the washbowl to interest him, and the bowl itself was cracked and badly riveted. He could only be doing this to spite her because she had torn him off a strip about Alexander.

The other woman stuck in doggedly, and in the end all Petra could do was keep her personal limit firmly in mind and refuse to let herself be needled into risking more money than she could afford to spend just to outbid Hugo Baron. She was the first to drop out of the contest, smarting in spirit, but with her finances intact as she left the pair of them to battle on.

The other woman eventually gave a dismissive wave of the hand in answer to the auctioneer's questioning look, and lot no. 152 was knocked down to Hugo.

Petra was wedged in by the crowd, and couldn't do what she would have liked to do—leave immediately. In any case, there were her purchases to collect and pay for. She had to wait there until the auction ended.

She was going out to the van for the last time when she was stopped by Hugo, who was carrying the washbowl and its contents.

'No need to gloat,' she said, getting in first with the smart words. 'Just go home and enjoy your petty triumph.'

'And what petty triumph exactly would that be?' he asked.

'I can think of no other reason for your buying that little lot than to get one up on me. If that's not petty, I don't know what is.'

'If that were my reason, then I would agree with you. But it was not. Didn't you pick up any of the signals I was trying to give you?'

'I saw all the frowns and glares you were directing at me, but I'm used to that. It certainly wasn't your attitude that made me drop out of the bidding. I'd reached my limit.'

'You can be incredibly silly at times,' Hugo said crushingly. 'I was trying to convey the fact that you could drop out of the bidding and leave it to me. I knew that the odds were that Maggie Taverner would go far further than you were willing to do, and I didn't want us to lose this little lot.'

'Us?' Petra asked with heavy irony. 'It seems to me that only one of us is walking off with the goods. However, it isn't a matter of life and death. Go home and enjoy your spoils. I'm not going to give you the satisfaction of moaning about it.' She turned away to her van, but he caught her arm with his free hand and stopped her.

'Listen, you hot-headed little idiot! I don't want to go home with anything but this.' He released her arm and picked a bit of shaped, tarnished metal out of the bottom of the bowl, which he then put down on the ground at her feet. 'The rest is yours, with my compliments.'

Petra, with the wind taken out of her sails, looked from the scrap of metal to his face suspiciously.

'Why should you want that? Or is this another weird mickey-taking operation?'

'This scrap of metal is an escutcheon from the *bonheur-du-jour*, the absence of which was the reason I got the *bonheur* at the price I did—and with as little competition. I saw it after you'd gone in to the auction, but I couldn't get across to tell you, so I just had to make sure that Maggie Taverner didn't walk off with the lot.'

Petra bit her lip, then shrugged and sighed. 'So, I owe you an apology, it seems. And more. I'll pay you for these, of course.' She touched the bowl with her foot.

'You don't need to. I shall more than get back what I paid in the increased value of the *bonheur*.'

She was suddenly too tired to fight him any longer. 'I won't argue now. We'll sort it out later. Meanwhile, thank you very much.'

He was staring thoughtfully at her. 'Do I really frown all that much?'

She allowed herself a small smile. 'Quite a lot. Most of the time you look ready to take on the world—only sometimes the world gets concentrated into one person...more often than not, me.'

'That doesn't sound very pleasant.'

'I manage to survive.'

The green eyes were still holding hers. 'Come and have a pub lunch with me,' he said surprisingly. 'As a peace offering.'

Petra looked at her watch. 'I have to be back at the shop. Manda's standing in for the morning.'

'It's only twelve. I can have you back by one. The morning can't be considered over until then.'

'And I've got all my stuff in the van. It hardly seems worth trundling off in two vehicles.'

He looked deep into her eyes. 'I think it is,' he said quietly. Then, before she could be frightened off by that, he went on, 'I want to talk to you about Alexander.'

Petra raised her eyebrows sceptically. 'It isn't long since you were telling me that Alexander was your business and nobody else's.'

'Opinions can be modified. It isn't long, equally, since I heard you telling Joe that all men were lousy bastards. I don't think you believe that a hundred per cent, either.'

Petra pulled a deprecating face. 'That was said in the heat of the moment. How on earth did you hear, anyway?'

'I was picking up your cast-off clothing.' He grinned at her. 'Poor Joe. He was the one to get more than he deserved, then.' He bent down and picked up the washbowl. 'Come on. We're wasting time. Let's put this in your van and be on our way.'

'I'm very low on petrol.' It was a last attempt to dodge lunch.

'You won't be using your van, except to get back to the shop afterwards. You can leave it here without inconveniencing anyone.'

Petra gave in, telling herself that if she had the chance of maybe doing Alexander a bit of good what else could she do?

They drove a mile or two out of Cheltenham to a quiet village pub of mellow Cotswold stone. Hanging baskets along its frontage were bright, even at this time of year, with winter-flowering pansies. There were very few midday customers, the tourist season being over, and Hugo settled Petra in an inglenook away from the group on stools at the bar before going over to order drinks and pick up a menu.

The menu was only a token gesture. After establishing that she wasn't allergic to shellfish, he told her that seafood mornay was the only possible choice for a discerning customer, with the landlady's home-baked french bread as accompaniment, and went back to order.

Petra sipped her vodka and tonic, watching him at the bar. What a strange mixture of a man he was. Tough as boots, and yet soft as putty. Worrying about his son as much as any mother would, and yet displaying all the steam-rollering insensitivity Alexander had told her about. Now that, willy-nilly, she was getting to know him better, she was finding that there was humour under that sometimes stiff, forbidding front he put up. And there was kindness going side by side with the high-handedness he could also display. What had made him like that? No fault in his upbringing, she was ready to swear. Mrs Baron must have been, and still was, a delightful mother, and though Hugo might protest about her he was still very fond of her, as the fiasco of a birthday party had shown. If he hadn't cared for his mother he wouldn't have bothered to have her over for a meal on her birthday, would he?

It was all very confused, and very confusing, and not calculated to make her feel she could be certain of saying the right thing as far as the business of Alexander was concerned. However, Hugo had said he wanted to talk to her. All she could do was listen and say what she truthfully thought.

He came back with the food, and for a while they gave full attention to the delicious mixture of white fish and shellfish in creamy sauce with its crunchy topping. Hugo had not forgotten the purpose of their being there, though. Eventually he put down his fork with a determined air and looked at Petra.

'I presume from Alexander's appearance when I found him in your shop yesterday that he had told you the sorry story of my mother's birthday?'

'He did,' she said cautiously.

'It was not one of the days I would care to repeat.' He looked keenly at her from under his forbidding brows. 'What did he say, exactly?'

Petra speared her last prawn and ate it, then put down her own fork. 'He told me the events of the day as he saw them. If you told me the story from your angle, the truth, I imagine, would be somewhere between the two accounts.'

'But closer to Alexander's version then mine. That goes without saying.'

Petra looked at him with some surprise. Did the man actually care what she thought? 'I didn't say that.'

'You didn't need to. Your succinct little lecture when I came to get him from the shop made your view quite clear. But I'll give you my version nevertheless.' He leaned back in his seat, the familiar frown drawing his eyebrows together.

Petra stretched forward and ran a delicate finger over the furrows.

'You're doing it again,' she said boldly.

A smile, surprisingly heart-warming, removed the frown, and Hugo began to speak.

'I was a little late bringing my mother back for the meal we'd planned, and we went straight in to eat. At that point all was well. Alexander was excited but normal. We had some of his favourite foods, and of course some of my mother's. We drank her health in champagne, Alexander toasting her in a weak version of Bucks Fizz for the first time and feeling rather grown-up about it. Then it was time to hand over her presents, and Alexander gave her his first.'

'Which pleased her?'

'Very much. Diorissima has always been her favourite perfume. Alexander had gone to town on the wrapping paper, spending hours sticking gold stars on to red paper. And he'd made her a home-made card, which pleased her no end. There were no problems at all at that point.'

'And what happened next?'

'I gave her my present—some Italian knitwear she'd had her eye on. So far so good. She loved that too.'

'And then?'

'And then we come to the bit that did not go according to plan.'

'The box . . .'

'Yes, the box. I'd had second thoughts about it.'

'Second thoughts? You?' Petra couldn't help saying.

His eyes held hers. 'Further reflection isn't beyond me. I thought Alexander had behaved amazingly well over the damned box. He had to understand just why he had to give up his wonderful find and start again on the present hunt. Not easy for a seven-year-old. But I'd managed to make him understand the reason, and he'd accepted it with good grace. I was proud of him. Apart from a few snuffles, he accepted the fair-play angle. Having thought long and hard about it, I decided that my mother should have the box after all, and know Alexander's part in the getting of it. I could well afford an extra for her in the circumstances, and Alexander deserved the glory of his find.'

Petra was silent for a moment, taking in the thinking behind what had seemed apparent insensitivity.

'But why on earth didn't you tell Alexander what you intended doing?' she asked.

'Because I wasn't sure right up to the afternoon of the birthday that I was going to be able to get the box back. Someone else was interested in it, and the man I'd sold it to was going to drive the hardest bargain he could. I actually secured it and picked it up on the way to collect my mother for her birthday party.' He looked challengingly at Petra. 'No doubt it will amuse you no end to hear that I had to pay twice what I sold it for to get it back again.'

Petra made no comment, but her opinion of him was undergoing something of a change. A man who could do all this was not the cold fish she had thought him to be.

'So you brought out the box...' she prompted.

'Exactly. Being careful not to steal the thunder of Alexander's personal present, you will notice. I was about to embark on the story of it and Alexander's star role—but my mother launched out into raptures as Alexander had rightly guessed she would. And Alexander bolted out of the house. In no time there was this almighty crash from the garden. The little blighter had done for my cold frame and most of my geranium cuttings, and was as defiant as hell about it, which somewhat diverted my mind from silver boxes. My mother didn't take kindly to the shouting match, which didn't stop her joining in with a few home-truths of her own before going home in high dudgeon once Alexander was in bed.' He shot a look at Petra. 'All right—I lost my temper. But I'm no saint.'

'That I had noticed,' Petra murmured. 'Why on earth didn't you tell Alexander that you weren't taking over his present, just moving heaven and earth to give him the pleasure of knowing that his grandma was getting the thing he wanted her to have?'

Hugo looked pityingly at her. 'Because by that time he was being sick, and you don't try to expound sweet reason to a child who is throwing up, if you'll forgive the crudity.'

'The morning after, then?'

'And risk getting him all worked up before going to school? Grant me a little common sense. Alexander had everything made clear to him last night. We now understand each other perfectly, and all is forgiven and forgotten.'

'Then that's all right,' Petra said rather lamely.

He looked hard at her. 'You find the explanation satisfactory?'

She flushed under his scrutiny. 'Why should it matter what I think? Alexander is the one who matters.'

'But you were concerned about Alexander. At least, that's what your outspoken opinion of my actions suggested.'

'Yes. I like Alexander. Very much.' She realised she was fiddling with her fork and put it down. 'But I find it a bit of a turn-around that you should pay any attention to what I think.'

'Perhaps I don't like anybody getting a totally wrong impression of my motives.'

She gave a brief laugh. 'You didn't give a tuppenny damn what I thought of your motives in trying to get me out of the shop.'

He looked steadily at her, unabashed. 'That was business. This isn't. Besides . . .'

'Besides what?' she said, filling in the pause.

'I know you a little better now.'

'And what does that mean?'

'It means that your opinion . . .' he paused, choosing his words carefully '. . . that your opinion has more weight than that of a stranger.'

'Even if I remind you of someone you disapprove of?'

He didn't look away from her. 'In spite of that.'

Curiosity got the better of Petra's discretion. 'Who is it—the person I remind you of?'

He pushed back his chair with a sudden impatient movement. There were sudden shadows now in the green depths of his eyes.

'No, Petra,' he said, gently still, but firmly. 'I invited you here for a specific purpose, but it wasn't to go into my past. I've told you what I want you to know.'

Petra, embarrassed, shrugged in pretended indifference. 'Sorry I spoke.'

'Time I was driving you back. It's ten to one.' They rose and left the pub, the short-lived drawing together over and an awkward silence between them again.

Petra sighed as she went back into Collections. That was the way it was destined to be between them, it seemed. A brief *rapprochement* followed by an estrangement that left them as far apart as ever, like some surreal dance.

What did it matter, though? she asked herself when Manda had left. She was only crossing Hugo Baron's path for a short time. By the end of January she would be off, seeking fresh fields and pastures new, and Granville Row could revert to its untroubled calm and respectability with no one making waves and asking undesired questions.

All the same, she kept feeling a stir of satisfaction throughout the rest of the day. Hugo Baron had cared what she thought about him. She didn't know why this should give her pleasure, but it did. He was not the unfeeling creature she had thought him. Today he had given a little of himself away. True—he had tried to take it back again pretty quickly, but he had not entirely managed to do so. She would not forget the brief, revealing time when he had cared what she thought.

# CHAPTER SIX

HUGO was letting himself into Granville Antiques at the same time as Petra came round to open up Collections next morning. She called a cheerful 'Hi!' and in return got the coolest of 'Good morning's with hardly a glance before Hugo disappeared into the shop.

Petra stared at the spot where he had been, taken aback. She ought to be used to it by now, this hot-and-cold manner of his, but after yesterday she really had felt that they were through the rough and on to smooth ground.

But no, it seemed. She was useful when he had the whim to consider her so, and not worth a pleasant conversational exchange otherwise.

'Well, sucks to you, you old misery,' she said under her breath. What did it matter to her?

Enough, it seemed, to put her in a less than sunny mood for the first half of the morning. She sold one or two small, easy things, but lost a big sale which might well have gone through if she had given her mind to it instead of brooding about her unpredictable neighbour. She gave herself a good talking-to and was rewarded just before closing for lunch at one o'clock by the sale of the fire-screen she had bought the previous day.

While she was in the little kitchen at the back of the shop, heating up some home-made soup to go with the ham rolls she had brought, there was a tap on the back door.

Petra opened it to find Hugo there. He glanced at the pan on the stove.

'I was counting on your coming out to eat with me,' he said.

'You're too late, I'm afraid.' Petra's manner matched the coolness of his earlier greeting. 'As you can see, I'm about to eat here.' And if she hadn't been he needn't think she was going to allow herself to be yo-yoed around in the way that seemed normal to him.

Instead of leaving her to it, he walked into the kitchen and leaned against the door through to the shop, watching her. The soup bubbled up in the pan and Petra dashed to save it, not quite making it. She got a cloth from the sink and wiped up the small amount of over-spill, then really looked at Hugo for the first time. There was an air of tremendous strain about him, she realised, and underneath his surface tan his skin had an almost grey cast to it.

'Are you all right?' she asked.

'I'm fine.' The words were patently untrue.

'You don't look it.' Her blue eyes scanned his face carefully.

'I just felt like company over lunch. There's nothing wrong with that—unless you think two days running makes it rather too much of a habit.'

She hazarded a guess. 'It's not Alexander again, is it?'

He seemed to resent her suggestion of vulnerability on the subject of his son. 'Forget it.' He straightened up and made for the door. 'Get on with your lunch. I'm holding you up.'

Petra stepped between him and the door. 'Look, why don't we share my picnic?' she said, relenting and pulling out a chair from the small table. 'There's plenty for two.'

'Of course there isn't. You weren't expecting anyone. In any case, I really couldn't care less about eating.'

'Don't be ridiculous. You've just asked me to come and eat. You'd have had something then.'

'Only for the sake of it. You go ahead. I'll watch.'

'Oh, no. I can't eat if you don't, and I'm ravenous!' she said threateningly.

He gave in and sat at the table. 'Just a little, then.'

She went and got a bowl from the china display in the shop.

'It's a good job you're not a milliner, or we'd be eating out of hats,' he said ironically.

When they had embarked on their soup, she asked casually, 'So what has Alexander been up to now? It is him, isn't it?'

Hugo put down his spoon. 'Not in the way you think. He has to go into hospital tomorrow to have his tonsils out.' His voice was doing a good job of being casual, but it didn't fool her. 'They phoned this morning to say he'd jumped to the top of the cancellation list.'

Petra studied his face, weighing her answer judiciously.

'Well, it's not exactly something to look forward to, but I presume it's considered necessary. They don't do that operation for nothing these days, do they?'

'It's certainly strongly advised. He's had so many ear and throat infections.'

'Then he'll be far better off having the operation, won't he?' she said encouragingly.

'That's the theory of it.'

She looked hard at him, then put a hand on his arm. 'Every parent has a few collywobbles at a time like this. I'm sure he'll be all right.'

His eyes were bleak as winter. 'Are you? I wish I could have a little of your confidence.'

She went on studying his face. 'There's something more, isn't there? I can't believe that someone like you would be thrown by what is after all a fairly routine minor op.'

'No operation is minor to us.' He managed to get out at last the fact that was tormenting him so much. 'Alexander's mother died under anaesthetic just over two years ago. They said it was an unexpected allergic reaction to one of the drugs used.'

Petra was very still. 'I see,' she said softly. 'And you're wondering if there's a possibility of Alexander having similar problems.'

His eyes met hers. 'I can deal with my own thoughts and fears. But Alexander knows what happened to his mother. It's his fear that I find so painful.'

'How did he find out?'

'Thank you for not saying, "It would have been more sensible not to tell him".'

'Of course you didn't tell him!' Petra said emphatically.

'No. He overheard. The police came to the house to tell me about Kate. It was mid-evening, and Alexander wasn't sleeping too well at the time. I'd taken the man into the drawing-room when it was obvious that he'd something serious to say. It was only when he stumbled to the end of it that I looked across the room and saw Alexander standing in the doorway, with a chalk-white face and eyes like dead coals. He looked like that this morning when the call came from the hospital. He doesn't say anything, and I'm damned if I know what I can say without making things worse.'

'Maybe it isn't a question of saying,' Petra said slowly. 'The best thing is for him to find out by experience that what happened to his mother is a million-to-one chance. Once he has got through this op, the trauma will have shrunk beyond recognition.'

'Exactly. It's getting through tonight that exercises my mind, though.'

Petra got up, breaking the tension. 'I think we'll forget the soup. It's gone cold now. But I expect you to do better with the ham roll.' She poured a mug of tea. 'Sugar?'

'No, thanks.' He drank deeply from the mug and picked up the ham roll.

'What the two of you need, I imagine,' Petra told him, 'is plenty of moral support. I should think Mrs Baron would be good at that.'

'The best. But unfortunately she's in bed with flu.'

'What rotten timing.'

'Couldn't be worse.'

They were silent for a moment, then Hugo's eyes sought hers.

'I may as well come clean. Alexander obviously regards you as a good source of moral support. I wondered if you might consider making a third for dinner tonight and helping us through the evening.'

Petra didn't have to think about her answer. 'Well—of course I will!'

He looked almost boyish in his relief. 'Really? I'd be eternally grateful.' He must have felt he was going a bit over the top, and made an effort to rein in his gratitude. 'I'm sure plenty of other people would show willing, but I'm trying to think of it from Alexander's point of view.'

'Of course,' Petra said gravely. 'I certainly wouldn't imagine that anyone else in the house wanted his hand held.'

He grinned. 'You know damned well that Alexander won't be the only one to be glad you're there.'

Petra felt a ridiculous surge of pleasure at his words. She hoped it didn't show. 'What we need to do,' she said, thinking on the hoof, 'is make it such a special night that Alexander hasn't a hope of thinking about tomorrow.' Her brow furrowed in concentration. 'Does he like fireworks?'

'Loves them—but it's a bit late for that.'

'That doesn't matter. We'll have the fireworks Joe and Manda and I never got round to using on the fifth. And what about a winter barbecue instead of sitting staring at each other round a table? Would that interfere with what your housekeeper has got planned?'

'A phone call can take care of that. I'm more concerned with whether the barbecue will work. It hasn't been used for ages.'

'Oh, you'll resurrect it.' Her eyes sparkled at him across the table. 'Am I being terribly bossy?'

'I think we can take it.' He smiled. 'The more distraction the better.'

'I can be very distracting when I choose,' Petra said.

'So I've observed.' His tone made her blush. She got up quickly.

'Well, that's that, then. Tell me what time to come, and where, and I'll be there.'

He gave her precise directions to his home—Abbotswood, off the Andoversford Road, near Whittington, and Petra said she would be there at six.

When Hugo had gone, she found herself not quite believing the changed direction of the day. The morning might have been off course, but the afternoon was something to sail through very sunnily. She rationalised her good spirits. It was because she was used to looking after someone, she told herself. All those years with her parents and their problems. And now Alexander. Yes, that was it. It was simply a matter of being glad that she was of use to someone again.

\* \* \*

Hugo and Alexander were out on the terrace when she drew up in front of the Cotswold stone manor house. Hugo came down the shallow steps to greet her, Alexander dancing around his heels like a puppy. Hugo looked different. He was wearing lived-in-looking cords tucked into green wellingtons, and a baggy Aran sweater. His hair was verging on unruly, and—surprisingly—it suited him.

'How's the barbecue behaving?' Petra asked as she got out.

'We've lit it,' Alexander said excitedly. 'I had to blow a bit, but it's fine now. And Mrs Dawson's left us pieces of meat in the yukkiest sloppy stuff I've ever seen.'

'Chicken in a marinade,' Hugo interpreted, ruffling his son's hair.

'And sausages and tomatoes and onions and beef-burgers and potatoes cooking in the oven, but we'll finish them off on the barbecue because I like the burnt bits,' Alexander chattered on. 'Have you brought the fireworks?'

'I have. And something else that I didn't intend bringing, I'm afraid.' Petra reached into the van and lifted out a plump tabby cat, who tucked her head under Petra's chin and purred loudly.

Alexander put up a hand to stroke the soft fur. 'Is she yours?'

'Almost. She belongs to my upstairs neighbours, but we share her quite a bit. She's called Ockie, short for Octavia.'

'There's got to be a reason for "Octavia",' Hugo said.

'Of course. Manda pulled her out of the canal where someone had thrown her as a kitten. So that was one of her nine lives gone from the start.'

Hugo groaned. 'Oh, dear! Octavia comes from the Latin for eight,' he told Alexander.

'I know that,' Alexander said in a lordly way. 'We've done about octagons at school.'

Petra's eyes met Hugo's and they laughed. 'So how come Ockie's in the van?' he asked.

'She must have stowed away back at the house. I hadn't a clue until I turned off for Whittington, when she miaowed in my ear and nearly sent me through the roof. Could I put her somewhere safe until I go home, and give Manda a quick ring to tell her where she is?'

'In my room, *please*, Daddy?' Alexander urged. 'She'll love the duvet on my bed. I know she will.'

This was the night when Alexander would be denied nothing.

'All right, as long as you take care of her toilet arrangements,' Hugo said.

'A cardboard box with plenty of newspaper in it will be fine,' Petra said. 'Ockie's very ladylike. Her only sin is a tendency to enjoy having kittens rather too frequently. This isn't all fat cat, by the way. It's a cat-and-kittens package.'

'Really?' Alexander ran a wondering, exploratory hand along Ockie's flank. 'You'd better carry her in, then, Petra.'

Petra noticed that Hugo didn't insist on his son's calling her Miss Collins this time. Progress was being made in the taming of the former stuffed-shirt Mr Baron.

While Hugo went to put meat on the barbecue, she followed Alexander into the house and up the panelled staircase to his room. In the hall she had caught a glimpse through an open door of rose-scattered chintz on soft, comfortable chairs, and the inevitable gems of antique furniture. But it was a homely home. There might be flowers in a copper bowl reflected on the polished refectory table, but there were also Alexander's shoes dwarfed by his father's on the parquet floor under the table. She liked, too, the paintings everywhere. In this particular field Hugo seemed to lean towards the modern, she noticed.

Ockie turned round the obligatory number of times, then settled down contentedly on Alexander's duvet. They saw to her mod cons, and then closed the door safely on her. 'But I'll come and see you soon, Ockie,' Alexander promised as the door was closing.

Ockie might turn into a very helpful prop tonight, Petra thought as Alexander directed her to the phone.

'Want me to come and get her?' Manda asked when informed of her cat's adventure.

'Not unless you're worried about her maternal state.'

Manda scoffed derisively. 'That one would have kittens on a clothes line without turning a hair.'

'Well, in that case, leave her with me. She's going to serve quite a useful purpose.'

'There's always a first time,' Manda said laconically. Petra knew she was mad about the cat, as they all were.

'You don't fool me. I'll look after her,' she said.

'Ask them if they want a kitten in due course. I've run out of people to give little Ockies to,' Manda said, and hung up.

Hugo looked up from the barbecue, which was smelling delicious. His eyes took in what Petra was wearing now that there was no distracting cat for her to hide behind.

'How about a run-down of the origins of tonight's finery?' he said.

'An Afghan wedding dress—red velvet with gold embroidery, and an absolute godsend for chilly November evenings outdoors,' she told him, giving a little twirl.

'Especially when worn over a black jumper and ski pants.' He had great powers of observation, since not much of either garment was on show.

Petra poked around on the barbecue. 'It looks as though you're doing a good job here. Shall we leave your father to it and go and organise the fireworks, Alexander?'

'What do you mean?' Alexander was puzzled. 'We usually light them on the terrace wall.'

'Not tonight. This is a fireworks display with a difference. We need to find special places in the garden where the fireworks will look best. Have you ever seen a Golden Rain through leaves?'

'No. Never.'

'Tonight you will. You can get the box out of the van if you like.'

When Alexander had gone racing off, she said to Hugo 'Is there anything in the garden you particularly worry about?'

He looked up at her, the glow of the fire giving his face the timeless look of someone in an old master painting.

'There's only one thing I'm particularly worried about tonight,' he said softly, 'and he doesn't grow in the garden.'

Petra touched his hand in swift understanding, and went off with Alexander to position the fireworks.

They ate by the light of candles in glass lanterns on the terrace, close to the barbecue to bask in its warmth. Hugo had made jugs of champagne cup, mixed with extra lemonade for Alexander, and he had run an extension from the house so that Handel's *Music for the Royal Fireworks* could play softly while they ate to prepare them for the display.

Petra began by giving each of them six giant sparklers to position to start the show, and they met up again after much rustling and laughter in the darkness.

Alexander's six sparklers were in tubs illuminating the edge of the terrace. Hugo's flared either side of a flight of steps across the lawn, showering cascades of sparks on rock plants and mellow stone. Petra's were tied to the branches of an apple tree, bringing the late fruit and gnarled branches to dazzling life against the dark sky.

In the show proper, flashes of colour highlighted old walls and sculptures. Foliage took on new, magical dimensions, and as a final triumph a group of Silver Rains created a fairy-tale reflection from the silent fountain in the centre of the pool.

'Wow! I never want ordinary fireworks again,' Alexander told his father happily.

Mention of bed as they went towards the house cast the first shadow.

'I don't like operations,' he said, his voice unsteady.

'Nobody does. But they're soon over, and I know you'll be brave,' Petra told him matter-of-factly. 'Ockie once had an operation, you know. Shall I tell you about it? It all began when she stole a chicken—a whole one.'

She walked upstairs hand in hand with the small boy, recounting an involved story of a bone in Ockie's throat while Alexander listened, spellbound.

'Could Ockie stay here a bit longer?' he asked when his father brought him back to the bedroom where Petra was waiting with the contented cat.

'I should think she might,' he said, raising a querying eyebrow in Petra's direction.

'I'm in no hurry,' she told them.

Alexander's arms went round his father's neck. 'Don't worry,' he said stoutly. 'Ockie and I will be quite all right.'

As they went downstairs, Hugo said quietly, 'I can't thank you enough for all you've done tonight.'

'Ockie's the real heroine of the hour,' Petra said.

'I'll settle for two heroines. Come and sit by the fire.'

Hugo pushed a deep settee closer to the log fire. 'What can I get you? Vodka and tonic, wasn't it?'

'Lovely.' Petra had discarded her boots before coming into the house. She tucked her slender bare feet up under her red velvet skirt on the settee, and watched Hugo getting the drink. She felt a little shy with him now that the focus of the evening had shifted away from Alexander. But she couldn't rush away before the little boy was lulled safely to sleep by Ockie's hypnotic purr.

Hugo put her drink on a small table near her, and stooped to put another log on the fire. The glow from the burning wood softened his strong features, re-minding her what a different person she had seen to-night. It was hard to realise that this was the cold, hostile man of their earlier encounters.

He brought his whisky over and sat at the other end of the settee, long legs stretched out towards the fire. Petra raised her glass towards him. 'Here's to tomorrow at this time, when all's safely over.'

'I'll drink to that.' His eyes held hers as they drank the toast. 'Tell me—how did you learn to handle people so well?'

'I don't know that I do. And in any case, as far as Alexander is concerned, Ockie's done the major job.'

'She was certainly there at the right time just now. What a stroke of luck that she had had an operation too.' He read Petra's sheepish change of expression. 'Or are you going to tell me now that she didn't?'

'I'm afraid you have to put that particular story down to poetic licence. We seemed to need a diversion and Ockie provided it.'

'You see?' he said triumphantly. 'You do know how to handle people. I would have floundered at that point.'

'That's because you have a strong subtext in your mind, while I have only the firm conviction that all will be well.'

He looked steadily at her. 'I'm glad you're here,' he said. 'It's good to hear statements like that.'

Petra felt again the wave of shyness that had gripped her when they first came into the sitting-room. She dragged her eyes away from his and looked round the pleasantly shadowy room, with its pools of lamplight and flickering firelight.

'This is a lovely room,' she said. 'It looks as though it's grown slowly into what it is. You know how some places look as though they've been ordered instantly by the yard and the ton?'

Hugo looked round reflectively. 'You're only part right. The furniture was collected over the years, admittedly, but it hasn't always been brought together in this particular room. Somehow, after the time when I was told about Kate in here, I had to change the place and remove the image of that night from my mind. So there was a grand reshuffle in the house, and this is how it turned out.'

'Since you've mentioned that night,' Petra said, 'I wondered after you told me about it why the police came into it. Couldn't your wife's doctor have told you far less shockingly?'

Hugo sipped his whisky, staring into the fire. 'As a matter of fact, I had no idea my wife was in hospital,' he said at last. 'She had left here several weeks before—and I didn't have a forwarding address.'

Petra wished fervently that she could withdraw her comment about the police, but it was too late now. She even wished that Hugo would do his usual retreat into unapproachability after telling her to mind her own business. But he didn't.

'I'm so sorry,' she said awkwardly. 'I had no idea.'

'Of course you hadn't. No one around here knew. Kate had spent as much time away as she had under this roof. They weren't to know that this time was any different.' Perhaps it was the strain of the evening before Alexander's operation. Whatever the reason, Hugo seemed uncharacteristically inclined to talk. He drained his glass and went over to refill it. 'She was an actress, you see. I believe, looking back, that marrying me was no more than another role among many.' His tone was cynical, hurt, and Petra ached for him. 'But the idea of a long run didn't suit Kate. She kept going back to the theatre, again and again. It didn't matter where, or how little she saw of Alexander. Every new set of grotty lodgings was magic, every day spent here just a waiting for something to happen. When she told me that she had accepted a year's repertory contract at the other end of the country, I decided that enough was enough. I told her that she had to choose between Alexander and me, and the theatre. She didn't hesitate over the choice. Presumably she felt there was still enough of a link for her to give my name as next of kin when she went into hospital.'

Petra heard his words, but more than anything she heard the hurt underlying them. She reacted instinctively, getting up and going over to him where he stood looking down into the flames, putting her hand on his arm.

'I wish I had never brought the subject up. I'm so sorry,' she said, her eyes luminous with feeling as she looked up at him.

'The subject, whether I like it or not, is very much in my mind tonight. And I mentioned Kate first, not you.' He took her hand and gave it a little squeeze before returning it firmly to her side. 'But that's enough of that.'

She wasn't sure whether he was referring to the subject, or to her impulsive gesture. She turned away awkwardly and sat down again, then almost immediately got up.

'I think, if you don't mind, I'll go and collect Ockie and be on my way, as long as Alexander is asleep.'

Hugo was staring down into the fire again. 'As you wish,' he said briefly.

Petra left him and went quietly upstairs. A couple of minutes later she was back in the sitting-room, minus Ockie.

'I'm afraid there's been a bit of a development up there,' she said, unsure whether to laugh, as she felt inclined, or to be embarrassed—as she was equally inclined.

'Is he all right?' Hugo asked, instantly alerted to Alexander.

'Fast asleep, but Ockie isn't. She's in the bottom drawer of Alexander's chest of drawers—it must have been left open. She's had two kittens on top of his jumpers, I'm afraid. We really had no idea when they were due, and she wasn't all that big so we assumed later rather than sooner. Two kittens explains that. Last time she had half a dozen.'

He looked at her with amusement. 'Life is never simple with you around, is it? Ask you for a meal, and one also gets a pregnant cat giving birth.'

They both laughed, Petra with relief.

'So what do we do now?' Hugo asked.

'I think, if you can bear it, it would be better to leave her where she is, at least until tomorrow. I'm a bit wary of handling the kittens so soon, and she'll stay put with them. She's a very good mother.'

'But a rather surprising house guest.'

'Actually,' Petra said, thinking ahead, 'it may not be a bad idea for Alexander to wake up to that sight tomorrow, don't you think? At least it will take his mind off less pleasant matters.'

'Pragmatist!' Hugo said. 'But I think you have a point. What about food for Ockie? There's cold chicken in the fridge.'

'If she gets that, and milk and water, she'll be your friend for life.'

'For tonight will do nicely,' he said drily. They went through to the kitchen and sorted out three bowls for Ockie. When they came downstairs again, Petra said daringly, 'If you let Alexander have the prospect of keeping one of the kittens, he'd have even more to occupy his mind. Something to look forward to beyond the op. What do you think?'

'I think you are an unscrupulous opportunist. But as a matter of fact he has been pleading for a pet, and I'm quite willing for him to have one. I'll put it to him tomorrow.'

'Oh, good! What a satisfactory arrangement.' Petra beamed. 'And now I really will be on my way.'

This time it was Hugo who made the impulsive gesture. He put his hands on her shoulders and leaned down to kiss her on the forehead.

'And I *wanted* to do that,' he said, reminding her wickedly of the last time he had kissed her. 'You've been a godsend tonight, for both of us. Thank you, Petra.'

'You're welcome,' Petra said, fighting down a blush, but warming in a different way to the genuine warmth of his voice. For once, the atmosphere hadn't deteriorated at the end of the encounter. Wonders would never cease.

Back at the house she ran up and knocked on Joe and Manda's door.

'No Ockie, I'm afraid. She gave birth in one of Hugo Baron's bedrooms. You've got a cat with a fine sense of place and timing there.'

Manda groaned. 'Oh, heavens! That's us a few rungs further down on the social scale in Mr B's opinion, I presume, then.'

'He took it like a lamb,' Petra said, still with a note of wonder in her voice. 'There were two kittens, and he's actually willing to keep one of them for Alexander. I left them all there. I wasn't sure how Ockie would react to being moved at this stage.'

'That's your story,' Joe said sceptically.

'I expect she just wanted an excuse to go back,' Manda grinned. 'Come on, own up, Petra. You're beginning to fall for your Mr Baron.'

'Of course I'm not!' Petra denied more vehemently than their teasing justified. 'I'd just rather get on with people than have constant trouble with them.'

Joe nodded. 'Just good friends?' he asked wickedly. 'I've heard that one before.'

'And for that you can fetch your own ill-mannered cat back,' Petra said vengefully.

Manda looked at Joe. '"The lady doth protest too much, methinks".'

'You are obviously both in a ridiculous mood. I'll wish you goodnight.' Petra proceeded with dignity down to her flat. Joe's voice floated after her.

'Doesn't she move well?'

'Practising for the big house,' Manda said.

Petra ignored them and let herself in to her own quarters.

Falling for Hugo Baron, indeed! Just because she had tried to help him through a bad time. How utterly ridiculous! She would have done the same for anyone.

*   *   *

The following day Petra had offered to deliver a large item to an address beyond the hospital where Alexander's operation should be safely over by the lunch-hour, which was when she set off. On impulse, she called in at a pet shop and bought a blue pottery bowl with 'Puss' on it. Alexander wouldn't be interested in anything in the way of food or drink for a day or two, but he might be pleased to have something for his kitten.

She signed a 'Get well' card and asked at the reception desk if she could leave it for Alexander Baron. The receptionist established her connection, then suggested that she take it up and leave it with the ward sister, saying that only parents were allowed to see a child on the day of an operation but a gift could be handed in.

At the door of the ward, a tired-looking, sleep-lacking Hugo was just coming out.

'Well?' Petra queried.

'He's fine.'

Petra's instant response was to fling her arms round him in a paroxysm of delight. 'Oh, that's wonderful!' she said, hugging him fiercely. In her demonstrative family, hugs and kisses were everyday currency, and the recovery of a child a most definite cause for rejoicing.

Thinking about it afterwards, she was not sure whether his arms tightened round her in initial response, or whether she had been so full of feeling herself that she had imagined it. What she knew beyond all shadow of doubt was that Hugo Baron, she was all too soon made aware, was standing like a statue, not responding in the least, as though her excess of emotion was disgusting him.

She stepped back. 'I'm very glad,' she said unnecessarily.

His face was empty of expression. 'So I gather. What are you doing here?'

'I brought a present for Alexander. And I was concerned to know how you both were, damn it!' she said accusingly, embarrassed to be made to feel an intruder, and an uncontrolled one at that.

He took her arm and turned her away from the ward towards the stairs. 'I think there is something that has to be said,' he told her, stopping to look her in the face. His eyes had grey tones in their depths again, she saw. 'Petra—I would hate you to get the wrong idea because of last night. I was grateful for your help—overwhelmingly so. And you are an extremely attractive woman. But I have no intention of getting involved with anyone else after my experience with Alexander's mother. Especially you.'

Petra felt blood rush to her face. She was appalled by the crude abruptness of his statement. It was too outspoken to be laughed off. And, in any case, the last thing she felt like doing was laughing.

She squared up to him. 'I'm here because of Alexander. I hugged you because I was pleased about Alexander—nothing more. But if you find that unnatural and displeasing, then I apologise.'

'Are you sure Alexander was all you were thinking about?' he said, blunt to the point of rudeness again.

'Well, of course I was pleased for you. Why shouldn't I be?' she said, but her words sounded lame in her own ears. The teasing she had taken from Manda and Joe the previous night, combined with Hugo's totally unexpected pronouncement on the same theme, made her awkward and unsure of herself. Just how had she been behaving to make everyone around jump to this conclusion?

She felt that he sensed her uncertainty, but, more surprisingly still, he went on to show that he shared it in some way.

'Perhaps I'm speaking to myself as much as to you,' he admitted stiffly. 'I've behaved out of character ever since you came on the scene. I have never asked advice or help from anyone, and I regret doing so now. But more than anything I regret that you were the one I turned to.'

'Why are you suddenly so anti-me?' Petra protested, stung to direct anger by his words. 'What do you mean— you have no intention to get involved with anyone, "*especially me*"? You regret turning to anyone, again "*especially me*"? What am I? An ogre?'

'Not an ogre. I have been perfectly honest with you. You are someone to whom I am drawn, and yet would do anything not to be drawn. Do you remember that I told you you reminded me of someone who had not...how did I put it?...had not brought me un-adulterated pleasure?'

'I do,' she said curtly. 'It's filed along with several equally unpleasant and unnecessary things you have said to me over the weeks.'

'Haven't you guessed who I meant? Then let me tell you. You are so much the same kind of person as Alexander's mother. To put it plainly, you are everybody's friend, but have no special commitment to anyone. Kate was like that. You want to be free to take whatever life puts in your path. Kate, in spite of her family, couldn't refuse any theatrical offer that came her way. Do you imagine I enjoy the fact that I find someone like you, like Kate, attractive? The old pattern emerging all over again? But this time around, thank heaven, I recognise the danger signals and I can act upon them. You are a beautiful, funny, gutsy woman—but you are not for me.'

Petra drew herself up in icy fury. 'Aren't you forgetting something? There are two people involved in this imaginary partnership of yours. You may have a

problem—but I haven't. So I'm sorry if I remind you
of your wife, and I'm certainly not flattered. But you
can rest easy. I haven't the least desire in the world to
take her place. Please give this to Alexander for me, if
you don't consider it will rock your precarious family
boat.' She put the bowl in his hand and looked stormily
at him. 'And don't worry. I shan't be around much
longer to tax your iron resolve. Until I leave Granville
Row, I'll do my level best to keep out of your way.'

Her outrage took her as far as her van, but once she
had slammed the door on the suddenly hostile world
Petra found herself shaking so much that she had dif-
ficulty putting the key in the ignition.

The insufferable big-head. How dared he make her
feel like this? All along the line she had disliked him,
hadn't she? From the very start there had been nothing
but hostility between them. Any reason for getting
together had been concocted by him, and now he was
almost accusing her of setting out to slip into Alexander's
mother's shoes.

She started up the van, but the windscreen was misted
over. She reached out to wipe it clear, but it was only
as she touched the glass and a hot, angry tear fell on
her outstretched arm that she realised it wasn't the windscreen, it was her own eyes.

It was only her pride that was hurt, she told herself
fiercely, wiping her eyes and refusing to let a second tear
follow the first. Nothing more than her pride. The man
didn't deserve that she should be upset. He was intol-
erable, hugely self-opinionated, and obnoxiously outspoken. She wished she had let his mother limp home
with her damaged ankle the best way she could, then
she would never have set eyes on her stuffed shirt of a
son.

# CHAPTER SEVEN

IT WAS not in Petra's nature to allow herself to remain cast down for long, and she was soon flinging herself into the social lead-up to Christmas with the greatest determination. What did it matter if one man considered her *persona non grata*? She needn't give him another thought. She had loads of other friends.

Her thoughts were not quite so easily disciplined, she found, though. The memory of that last meeting with Hugo Baron recurred with annoying frequency, allowing her to imagine a hundred better ways in which she could have handled the situation. But it was useless to brood about past problems. A fresh one was approaching.

On the sixth of December the choir which Petra had joined shortly after moving into her aunt's old house was due to give a Charity Concert in aid of Shelter. The venue had only recently been mentioned, and it had rocked Petra back on her heels when she heard it. The concert was to take place in Hugo Baron's house, Abbotswood.

After mulling things over for a bit, Petra decided defiantly that she was not going to modify her private life because of him. She would not allow herself to drop out of the choir for the occasion. She would go and sing her heart out, and if he felt annoyed to see her under his roof again that was his problem, not hers.

The evening of the sixth, nevertheless, found her a little apprehensive, but determined to go through with the performance.

The choir members were taken to Whittington by coach to minimise parking problems. Cars were bumper to boot along the lane and drive to the house, and the house itself shone like a beacon with light streaming from every window across the snow-dusted lawns and terrace.

Mrs Baron was there, shepherding the girls of the choir through to the sun lounge at the side of the house where they were to leave their coats. Petra made no attempt to draw attention to herself, and Mrs Baron, caught up in her organising, didn't pick her out from the crowd of girls in long red skirts and white high-necked blouses.

Petra adjusted the crisp red moiré bow holding back her long hair, collected her candle lantern and music, and followed the line of singers out into the big hall where they were to group on and around the wide staircase. Through the open double doors of the main rooms she could see the seated audience—upwards of a hundred people. Candles were burning everywhere in readiness for the start of the carols, and at a sign from the choir's conductor the main lights were dimmed.

Petra heaved a quick sigh of relief. She hadn't yet seen where Hugo was, and in the semi-darkness now it was unlikely that she would be able to pick him out from the mysterious shapes of the audience. As she raised her candle lantern to waist height in unison with the rest of the choir, she knew that the flickering golden light would cast shadows and highlight over the planes of their singing faces, making it hard in return for anyone to recognise a member of the choir. She was safe for the first half of the concert. This was the half she most cared about, because she had to sing a minor solo part in one of the carols, and she didn't want to be put off by the sight of a hostile face. In the second half of the concert the lights would have to be on for the audience to read

the words of the carols in which they were to join, but
by then it wouldn't matter.

The programme began with 'The Seven Joys of Mary',
then old favourites like Peter Cornelius's 'The Kings' and
Tchaikowsky's 'Crown of Roses' alternated with lesser
known modern works. Petra almost managed to forget
who was among those listening to the music in the joy
of singing.

Her solo came in the last item of the first half. The
choir led in with soft humming of one verse and chorus
of 'Joseph Dearest, Joseph Mine', and it was while this
was happening that one of the candles in a branched
candlestick on the piano at the side of the hall flared up
wildly. Someone stepped forward from the shadowed
opening to the sitting-room, and just before the rebel
flame was extinguished Petra saw Hugo's face in its flare
of light.

She wished that had not happened, but she was professional enough not to let the tremor that ran involun-
tarily through her reach her voice. Sweet and pure, it
rang out clear as a bell. 'Joseph dearest, Joseph mine,
help me cradle the child divine...' She completed her
solo flawlessly, and the carol took its well-loved course.

Applause rang out, and a buzz of chatter, over which
Petra heard the high young voice of Alexander. 'Oh,
look! It is Petra. I told you so.'

Hugo was on his feet then, addressing the audience
in his deep, authoritative voice, telling them that mulled
wine was to be served and inviting the choir to get rid
of their lanterns temporarily and come back for their
own glass of wine.

When Petra returned, somewhat warily, Alexander was
waiting for her, cradling a glass of deep red wine in both
hands, which he placed carefully into hers.

'Thank you, Alexander. How are you now? Better, I hope?'

'Quite better. But I haven't been back to school yet. Daddy said not until after Christmas.'

'Very wise of him. Too many colds around at the moment.'

'You were singing, weren't you? I thought it was you, but you looked different with the candle under your face. Daddy thought so too. He said "Good lord! So it is!" when I told him. I think he was very surprised.'

I bet he was, Petra thought. Alexander was tugging at her sleeve.

'Petra, come upstairs with me. There's something I want to show you.'

Petra followed him up to his room, glad to have a legitimate reason to go to earth during the interval. She was shown a cat bed, ready and waiting for the much-longed-for kitten, and duly admired it. Alexander surprised her when he looked up and said suddenly, 'Do you know that I'm being sent away for Christmas?'

'No, I didn't know. Where? Somewhere nice?'

'I suppose so. The Bahamas, with Grandma. It won't be very Christmassy, though, will it? Grandma says it will be up to us to make it Christmassy, but how do you do that with no snow? Daddy isn't coming either.'

Petra tried not to let her disapproving surprise at hearing this show. 'Perhaps your father wants a rest,' she said carefully, aware that the subject was sensitive for the small boy.

'He won't rest. He's working. Decorators doing things all over the place because of new people taking over property, he says. Stodging, I say.'

He looked wickedly at her, and they both burst out laughing at the word. At that precise moment, Hugo Baron appeared in the doorway of his son's bedroom.

'So here you are,' he said, and could have been speaking to either of them. He was wearing a richly brocaded waistcoat in maroon and dull gold under his charcoal suit, and against her will Petra acknowledged once again what a good-looking man he was.

'Good evening, Petra,' he said with a brief smile, as though there had never been such a thing as that unpleasantly embarrassing business at the hospital.

'Good evening,' she said, getting to her feet and smoothing her skirt nervously. She felt decidedly awkward, and wished she had never followed Alexander upstairs to be tracked down in his room like a trespasser by this man who no doubt wished her miles away.

'Alexander—could you take Petra's glass downstairs? I believe they are being collected up,' he said, taking the still-warm goblet from her fingers and handing it to his son.

'I'll take it myself,' Petra said hurriedly, but too late.

'Alexander will be quicker. He's been helping all evening. I don't know how the Shelter committee would have managed without him.'

The small boy flushed proudly and marched off, full of importance. The bedroom seemed to shrink around Petra. She moved towards the door, but Hugo moved at the same time and managed to bar her way without giving the impression that he was doing it deliberately.

'I didn't know that you included singing among your talents,' he said, looking down at her.

'Only a small talent. I can at least keep in tune,' she said dismissively.

'A modest understatement. I had quite a surprise when I realised who the persuasive Mary was.'

Petra tackled head on the matter that was dancing around in her mind. 'Not a very pleasant surprise, I imagine. But I can't help being here. I've belonged to the choir ever since I moved here. The idea of dropping out because of tonight's venue wasn't really on.'

'It would have been ridiculous. Why on earth would it occur to you to do any such thing?'

She looked at him in hostile accusation. 'You surely can't claim that after our last encounter either of us would have wished for this evening. I certainly didn't. However, it's half over now. One more half of the programme, and I'll be on my way.'

'Aren't you being a little over-dramatic?' he said with an irritating smile. 'I can surely cope with you as a member of a thirty-strong choir.' He was making fun of her, and Petra didn't see the least bit of humour in the situation. She felt that her cheeks would soon match the bow in her hair, and the crimson skirt her fingers were still pleating with a will of their own.

'I must go down,' she said hurriedly. 'We have to assemble in the sun lounge for the start of the second half.'

'And I must make sure that the audience is in place again.'

The descent of the stairs was swift, Petra's feet skimming the surface in her haste to get away from him. As she lost herself in the milling choir members, she was heartily thankful that she didn't have to sing alone again.

This time, Mrs Baron was on the look-out for her.

'Petra! How fortunate that you are here!' she said. 'I've one or two bits and pieces for you to put into stock at the shop. I had a good clear-out of cupboards while I was getting over flu, and vaguely thought of the W.I. Jumble Sale, but then I realised that one or two things might interest you. Stay behind after the concert, will you, and look through to see what you fancy?'

'It's very good of you,' Petra said warily, 'but I'm in the coach with the rest of the choir, so I shall have to leave with them.'

'That doesn't matter. There'll be loads of people going your way. I can easily fix a lift for you.'

'Could your son perhaps bring the things to the shop? That would save bothering anyone for a lift tonight.' Petra had absolutely no desire to stay on at Abbotswood for a second longer than necessary.

'That was what I meant to happen, and why I brought the box over here with me tonight. But he's taking Alexander and myself to the airport tomorrow, then staying on in London for a few days, apparently. I know you'll be busy in the shop with the Christmas trade, so it makes sense for you to have all the stock you can. After Christmas, no one will want to buy anything for ages.'

'Petra——' Someone thrust a pole from which her lantern now hung into her hands. 'Come on. We're ready.'

'I'll see you afterwards,' Mrs Baron said, the matter settled as far as she was concerned. Petra resigned herself to an unwanted extension of the evening, and, to the singing of 'Masters in this Hall', the choir led off to process through all the rooms of the house before taking up their position on the stairs again.

In the event, it didn't seem that the evening was going to end too awkwardly. Mrs Baron kept Petra waiting a while, while the inevitable last-minute goodbyes and words were exchanged, but then she left the rest of the charity committee to do the honours and took Petra upstairs. Hugo had already disappeared towards Alexander's quarters, presumably well out of the way, seeing that his son got to bed.

There were rather more things to look through than Petra had anticipated, and Mrs Baron's stories of where each item had come from and what it reminded her of slowed down the selection process.

When they came downstairs again everyone seemed to have gone apart from Hugo's daily housekeeper, who was waiting patiently by the front door, coat and boots on.

Hugo appeared from the sun lounge with Petra's blue cape.

'Ready now?' he said. 'Then we'll be off, ladies.'

Petra slipped into her cape, disconcerted to find that her lift home was to be provided by Hugo, and heartily glad that the housekeeper would be travelling with them.

Her relief soon evaporated when Hugo turned the car in the opposite direction to the one in which her own house lay, and it became evident that the housekeeper was to be dropped off first.

Hugo took Mrs Dawson to her door, holding her arm on the snowy path, and when he came back to the car Petra told him, 'I didn't anticipate that you would have to turn out and take me home. I understood that I was to go with someone from town.'

'So you were, but I told them that I would take you,' he said calmly, executing an expert three-point turn in the far too narrow lane. 'I wanted to talk to you.'

'Again? I thought we'd said it all last time,' Petra said caustically.

'Yes, again.' He glanced down at her. 'You seem to have got a trifle confused about our last conversation.'

'Because I turned up at your house tonight? Don't worry. I shall be well and truly away from here by the time next year's concert comes round, if you're thinking of hosting it again.'

'Not because of tonight,' he said with exaggerated patience. 'Because of the way you're reacting to what I said.'

'How on earth do you expect me to react? You didn't exactly give the impression you wanted me around. Surely you're not claiming I'm mistaken about that?'

'But you are. I don't in the least object to your being around. I merely didn't want you to get the wrong idea about what might *develop* from your being around.'

Petra had an overwhelming urge to bang him on his conceited head with her music case.

'The wrong idea was in your head, not mine,' she said firmly. 'Until you came out with that appallingly embarrassing diatribe in the hospital, nothing of the kind had entered my mind. It can only be a product of your over-inflated ego if you think every woman you meet is going to be bowled over by your charms. Charms——' she added scathingly '—which, as far as I am concerned, have been more conspicuous by their absence than their presence.'

He gave a low laugh. 'So that's all right, then. I stand secure from all threat, safe in the defences of my charmlessness. But if that is the case, why have you gone to such lengths to avoid me?'

'Oh, for heaven's sake!' Petra exclaimed. 'What on earth is all this about? You warned me to keep my distance. That's exactly what I've been doing.'

'Wrong again. Once more—what I wanted was to make sure that you didn't develop the wrong idea about the way we were brought together by the circumstances of Alexander's illness. I thought it only fair to make that clear.'

'Which you did. So that's that.' Petra gazed out at the passing snowy landscape. She could have been looking at a boiling-hot desert for all her eyes took in.

'You are only able to have a friendship with a man if you think it likely to lead to something else, then?' he asked with interest.

'Of course not!'

'Then why avoid me? You see! You did misunderstand me. I wasn't saying that I never wanted to see you again. So there is no need to duck back into the shop when you see me in Granville Row, or wait until I drive off in my car before venturing out to yours.'

He had seen her avoiding action. Petra smarted under the humiliation of it. But they were turning into Oak Lane now, and the four-square shape of Oak House, lights on on the first and second floors, gave her courage.

'Well, that's that cleared up, then,' she said decisively.

'And, since neither of us has designs on the other, we can remain friends?'

She gave him a scathing look. 'Wouldn't that be better rephrased as, "We can become friends"? We don't seem to have done very well so far in that respect.'

'All right. Become friends, then. And no hard feelings?'

He offered a hand, and, after a second's hesitation, she put hers into his firm clasp.

'Good. Goodnight, then, Petra.'

'Goodnight.'

His sheer audacity had sledge-hammered her into acceptance of how he now appeared to see their relationship, but once she was in the house the spell of his forcefulness was broken, and Petra was angry with herself for being manipulated so easily.

Oh! That man! He had it coming to him. And not just for tonight. There was that never-to-be-forgotten business of making her go into his snobby restaurant in her jeans. She had been all set to pay him back for that, but the various crises about Alexander had side-tracked her.

Yes. She definitely owed him one. But how did you manage to get one up on someone who seemed to have the knack of always turning the tables on you?

She went to bed brooding on it, and, as was often the way, her obliging subconscious came up with an idea that had her grinning wickedly as she awoke. Oh, yes! What a beauty of a plan! If only it worked. She would jolly well *make* it work.

She was quite casual when she saw Hugo outside the shop on his return from London.

'How was the big city?' she asked him.

'Crowded, and well illuminated. How about this place? Business all right?'

'Fine.' She smiled at him, radiating safe friendship. 'Hugo, after our last talk, I feel a bit of an ass. Can I attempt to prove myself? Since we're friends, how about coming to a party with me, just to show that we both mean what we say?'

'Sounds like a pleasant idea. Whose "do" is it?'

'Some friends in Winchcombe. They usually give a fancy-dress party at this time of year. It's on the fourteenth. But perhaps you're booked then. It's a busy time of year.'

'No—I'm free. What's the theme of this extravaganza, then?'

'No particular theme this year. Wear what you like.'

'What about you?'

'I haven't decided yet. I'll come up with something.'

'Shouldn't be difficult. Your clothes often have a touch of the fancy dress about them, haven't they?' He eyed the traditional ex-service sailor jacket she was wearing over a long navy-blue skirt, then took in the crimson beret that gave a saucy finishing touch to the outfit. 'Still, I have to concede that that particular combination works very well. What time do you want to be picked up on the fourteenth?'

'Around half-past eight would be fine.'

'I'll be there.'

They went their separate ways, and once in the shop Petra hugged herself and squealed with glee, whirling from one end of the showroom to the other. She had got him! Like taking candy from a baby, she had got him!

She was ready and waiting in good time on the evening of the party, her highly useful blue cape covering her from shoulder to toe. She schooled her face into friendly greeting as she went to the door in answer to the ring of the bell at just before eight-thirty.

The Laughing Cavalier, but with Hugo Baron's face, stood on the doorstep. His brocade coat was full-skirted, what she could see of his shirt lace-trimmed. Knee-breeches left shapely calves in white hose on display. In his big-brimmed hat was a cockade of spectacular feathers.

Petra felt a surge of triumphant laughter threatening, and quickly suppressed it.

'How splendid!' she told him. 'You've really gone to town.' Then, with surprised honesty, 'It suits you, Hugo!'

He preened a little. 'It feels strangely easy on me. Perhaps I had a previous incarnation in Restoration times. I draw the line at this, though.' He was carrying the hat. He reached for her cloak. 'What are you wearing under this thing?'

Petra whisked teasingly away towards the car. 'You'll have to wait and see.'

'Something Tudor, I'd guess.' He was looking at her hair, the arranging of which had been given considerable thought. She had plaited seed-pearls into the side-pieces and swept them round to a clasp at the back of her head, capping the crown demurely, while below the plaits her shining hair ran riot as usual. His words proved that he was thinking just what she wanted him to think.

She gave him directions to her friends' house, and they drove off towards Winchcombe.

After a few moments, Hugo glanced sideways at her as the car purred along.

'I'm glad you invited me to partner you this evening.'

'Are you?' she said cautiously, adding, almost as an afterthought, 'Good!' How long would he stay in that frame of mind?

'It clears up our little misunderstanding very satisfactorily.' A pause. 'I am really quite fond of you,' he went on, startling her with the unexpected and most unlikely revelation. 'That was why I didn't want any wrong emphasis to creep into things.'

'Hugo—have you been drinking?' she blurted out. He did not, as he might well have done, resent the question.

'I'm stone-cold sober, and in my right mind in case you go off on that particular tack next. Does one have to be drunk or demented to enjoy your company?'

'There are times when it could help,' Petra muttered. She was beginning to get cold feet about tonight. Why on earth did Hugo—rude, unpleasant Hugo, as she knew only too well he was capable of being—why did he have to choose this particular moment, just before she dropped him right in it, to start saying nice things to her? Had tonight really been a good idea, or was it just a silly-clever return to childishness that ill became her?

They were arriving at the party venue and it was too late for second thoughts. They parked in the already crowded courtyard, and Petra held her cloak nervously around herself as she got out of the car.

Hugo smiled down at her. 'You won't be able to keep your secret much longer,' he said.

She drew in a big breath and put a hand on his arm as he reached into the car for the feather-bedecked hat.

'I shouldn't bother with that,' she said, then looked up at him, coming to a decision. 'Hugo... this isn't a fancy-dress party.'

In the middle of locking the car, he went suddenly still, then turned slowly to face her.

'I don't understand. You told me it was.'

'I didn't. You assumed it.'

He was silent, rethinking her invitation and their subsequent conversation.

'If I did, it was because you meant me to do so. Don't deny it. I remember that little exchange very clearly. I was misguided enough to be somewhat pleased by it.' His tone sharpened. 'Come on, own up. You wanted me to jump to the wrong conclusion, didn't you?'

Slowly Petra nodded.

'Why?'

Petra hesitated. Suddenly it seemed so cheap, so childish. Hugo saved her the necessity of answering.

'By God! It was because of that night at Quaglino's, wasn't it? You've been nursing a grievance ever since then—just biding your time. You set me up, you little she-devil, didn't you?' His eyes were glittering in the light of the outdoor spot-lamp.

She swallowed. 'Well—I'm un-setting you up now. We can go back for you to change. Nobody's seen you.' Nervously she added, 'In fact, I wouldn't really blame you if you went home—period. I—I'm suddenly feeling rather stupid.'

'But the idea was that I should look stupid, wasn't it?' He looked inscrutably down at her, then moved, taking her by surprise, and caught hold of her arm in a firm grip. 'Come, come, Petra. You don't really expect me to turn tail and run, looking as noble as this, do you? My Cavalier predecessors would cry shame.' He was propelling her towards the door. More people had arrived, and now they were no longer alone to sort out her lead balloon of a joke.

'You'll be the only one dressed like that,' she warned unnecessarily.

'Uniqueness is not unknown to me,' he said smoothly. 'Come along, my subtle little schemer. Don't hang back. You are about to have your pound of flesh.' His head bent closer to hers and he whispered in her ear, 'And may it give you the worst bout of indigestion you have ever suffered.'

Julia was in the hall to welcome them. She was wearing a bright yellow catsuit and what looked like a ton of beads. Who knew where ordinary dress ended and fancy dress began? Petra wondered wildly.

Julia's eyes roved over Hugo's splendour with interest.

'How nice that you could fit us in. You're obviously going on somewhere else later? Aren't you going to introduce us, Petra?'

Petra attempted to snap out of her tongue-tied embarrassment—the role she had so wrongly envisaged for Hugo—and did the necessary.

Hugo, radiating self-confident charm, refused the easy way out offered by Julia.

'I'm afraid we had a little misunderstanding over the nature of your party,' he told their hostess. 'And I was just too lazy to go back and do something about it. After all, having hired all this——' he fingered the lace of his jabot '—it seems a waste not to wear it. Do you mind? Do I embarrass you?'

'Not in the least,' Julia said, her eyes responding to the charm in his. 'I think you look perfectly splendid.'

'I don't really think my partner is of the same opinion. I rather think she wishes she were elsewhere.' He helped Petra off with her cloak, surveying her lengthily. Her dress was knee-length, the skirt and big sleeves of copper and black embossed taffeta, the bodice black velvet with a low, square neckline.

Hugo turned back to Julia. 'Doesn't she look charming? Perhaps I should attempt to make myself look a little more twentieth-century—remove a furbelow or two. I believe Petra would feel better about things if I did.'

Petra, cheeks burning, seemed incapable of speech.

'If you really want to "adjust your dress",' Julia said with a saucy smile, 'do use our room—first on the left at the top of the stairs.'

'Coming up to supervise, darling?' Hugo asked Petra with a glittering, wicked look.

'I think you are well able to look after yourself,' she said with feeling, and drew back into a recess in the hall to wait for him.

When he appeared again at the top of the stairs, he had removed his full-skirted coat and lacy jabot, and unbuttoned the narrow-banded neck of his shirt. Now, in the decidedly flattering knee-breeches and glossy boots, with the dash of the full, tightly cuffed sleeves of the snowy white cambric shirt, he looked pirate-like and infinitely more interesting and attractive than any other man there. He walked slowly and calmly down to her—knowing it.

'Shall we go in?' he asked, and proceeded to enjoy himself at the party as though nothing untoward had happened.

Once again Petra's idea of what kind of man he was had been turned upside-down. She would have expected, at the very least, a bit of aloofness. But no. Hugo was attentive, friendly both to herself and to everyone else—a charming, but at the same time worrying partner.

People began to dance, Petra and Hugo among them.

'Penny for them?' he asked at length, questioning her quietness as they moved around the floor with the easy harmony she remembered so well from the Quaglino's evening.

Petra looked up at him a little sheepishly. 'I'm wondering when you're going to turn nasty.'

'Keep on wondering,' he said with a calm smile. 'I'm not averse to the idea of your suffering a bit of doubt and trepidation.'

'It was only tit for tat, Hugo. You wouldn't deny anyone a fair retaliation, would you?'

'I'd dispute the fairness. I made you something of a Third World heroine, as I remember. Your aim was to make me look a fool.'

'Well, I didn't manage it, did I? You're the generous-spirited good sport everyone admires.' She looked up at him. 'You even——'

'Even what?' She had hesitated.

'You even look pretty good in the remains of your fancy dress.'

'You're not the only one who can improvise. But flattery's not going to get you anywhere, so save your effort for your dancing.' His long legs elaborated on the beat of the dance, and she followed his lead effortlessly, and with pleasure. In dancing there were no problems between them.

Or were there? she asked herself a little later, finding rather too much illicit pleasure in his close hold during a slow number. She eased herself guiltily away. Hugo looked down at her questioningly, but she turned her head aside and he relaxed his hold on her without saying anything.

They left the party at one o'clock, and Hugo had still not turned nasty.

'I wish you would explode and get it over with,' Petra told him as they drove down the steep road that skirted Cleeve Hill. The sky seemed to be all round the car, velvety dark and brightly studded with stars.

'What an apprehensive creature you're turning into. Not at all like the fighter you've been up to now,' he taunted.

'That's because all this amiability isn't much like you, either,' she retorted with spirit. 'Especially in tonight's circumstances.'

'You'll just have to accept that I have hidden depths of pleasantness as yet unplumbed.'

He went on keeping her guessing until they drew up beneath the dark windows of Oak House. In his Cavalier costume, Hugo looked like a ghost from a past century as he came round to open the door for Petra.

'I'm not asking you in,' she said hurriedly as she got out.

'I'm not expecting you to.'

He stood waiting while she sought the suddenly wayward keyhole and fumbled her key into it. The moon came out from behind a cloud, turning the pearls in the darkness of Petra's hair dazzling white as she looked up and said hesitantly, 'Goodnight, then. And—sorry.'

The air seemed to shimmer around them with its heady blend of starlight and moonlight . . . and some other less identifiable ingredient that sent a tingle down Petra's spine. She felt momentarily dizzy, and closed her eyes.

Did she reach out to him? She didn't know. But he was suddenly gripping her arms, steadying her.

He looked down at her, and the air trembled. Then his grip slackened and he stood back. 'That's it for tonight, Petra,' he said coolly. 'Whatever you're waiting for, you're going to be disappointed.'

Her eyes flew open to stare at him, but before she could answer he was leaping into the car and driving off with a squeal of tyres.

Petra's dizzy mind cleared slowly. Had he been referring to her waiting for the 'turning nasty' that she had spoken about? Or had he been implying that she was waiting for something quite different, her eyes closed, her face vulnerably uplifted?

Her mind went into a spiral again, and she relived that warning sensation, the one that had made her draw away from Hugo while they were dancing, back at Julia's.

It was his fault that such thoughts crept into her mind. He was the one who had given birth to them just now...shifted their relationship on to a plane where neither of them wanted it to be.

She drew her cloak around her, shivering a little in the frosty moonlight, the icy coldness of the ground striking through the thin soles of her flimsy shoes. Then she went into the silent house and closed the door on the bewitching night.

One thing was becoming clear. It seemed impossible for Hugo Baron and herself to be together without her thoughts wandering along crazy, forbidden paths. Paths across which he had put so firm and impassable a barrier.

Well, there was only one answer to that problem. She must stay away from him.

# CHAPTER EIGHT

'I DON'T think so. Sorry,' Petra told Hugo the following Wednesday when he suggested that she should join him for lunch.

'Busy?'

'Very. For which I'm thankful.'

'How about tomorrow, then?'

'I don't think so, Hugo,' she repeated steadily.

'What's the excuse for tomorrow?'

'No excuse. I just don't really want to have lunch with you.' There was no point in beating about the bush.

He picked up a paperweight and examined it, then put it down again. 'That's nothing if not straightforward. May I ask why you've suddenly gone off on a different tack? Last Saturday you were all for proving what friends we could be.'

Petra debated her answer. I've changed tack because I'm afraid of being with you. Because I'm not too sure that I am capable of being simply friends with you. Because you're too dangerous, even in small doses. None of the answers that surfaced in her mind satisfied her pride.

'Because. . .' She was suddenly inspired. 'Because the score's even now, isn't it? No need to spend any more time together.'

He stared at her. 'And that was the only reason you made a show of friendship?'

'Why else? Look at our short history realistically, Hugo.' She was warming to her fictional theme now. 'There hasn't been much of a friendly atmosphere most

138

of the time, has there? Why pretend? You're not really my kind of person, and I'm certainly not yours. What's the point of flogging away at a non-existent friendship? We're two people brought together by circumstances which aren't going to go on much longer. Let's leave it at that.'

'And Alexander is merely a victim of those circumstances, is he?'

Petra's eyes fell. 'I'm genuinely fond of Alexander,' she said quietly.

'I wonder if he will understand your kind of genuine fondness—there one minute, and gone the next?' he asked cuttingly. He took a postcard from his pocket. 'This was enclosed in a letter from my mother. Alexander finds writing a chore, so judge your rating in his world from that.'

Petra took the card. A sun-bright beach was pictured on one side of it. Alexander's laborious script filled the other. Little details of his days, questions about his kitten, 'see you when I'm back' bringing his message to a close.

'He hasn't written to anyone else,' Hugo said. 'Shall I tell him there's no point in writing to you either, since the Barons are not "your kind of person"?'

Her blue eyes looked levelly at him. 'It's no use trying to get at me through Alexander, Hugo. That's a dirty trick. Much though I like him, he's a child. He'll forget me in no time.' She hoped desperately that he would. Hugo's small son had made a strong claim on her affections. But what could she do about it?

'We Barons don't forget anything very easily, I'm afraid,' he said. Then his tone changed. 'But neither do we cry over spilt milk. That's that, then. Don't feel you can't come next door for drinks with all the rest of the Row on the twenty-first. It would look a little pointed if you didn't. And you know how hot I am on appearances.'

She had received a little card from Granville Antiques inviting her to a Christmas drinks party for all Hugo's tenants. 'I think I can manage that,' she said calmly.

'Good. I won't hold you up any longer, then.' He left.

She stared aimlessly round the shop after he had gone. In spite of the fir branches and red ribbons and coloured baubles decorating the place, and the Christmas lights she could see out in the Row, in her heart it had never felt less like Christmas.


'You're looking peaky,' Manda told her when they met in the entrance to Oak House later in the week. 'Are you all right?'

'I'm fine,' Petra said. 'Just tired. At this time of year, aren't we all?'

'As long as it's not that Baron man getting you down . . . We don't seem to have heard much about him recently.'

Petra shrugged indifferently. 'Nothing to tell you.'

'I suppose that's better than all you had to explode about a few weeks ago.'

Petra supposed it was. Why didn't it feel better, then?

'Going out tonight?' Manda probed.

'No.'

'Why don't you come up and have supper with us, then? I've come to the end of my Christmas party frock orders. All I have to do now is stop those dratted kittens of Ockie's sleeping on designer silk and satin before the women who've ordered them collect them.'

'I don't think so, Manda. Thanks all the same.'

'Your last chance before Christmas. We're off early to stay with Joe's mum until the day after Boxing Day. I've got a good, hot curry on the go.'

'Not even for one of your curries, I'm afraid.'

Manda looked hard at her. 'You *are* tired, aren't you? And your business sense isn't too lively, either. Do you know our rent for this month is almost three weeks late? I haven't forgotten—just been bogged down with work. I'll bring you a cheque down later.'

'Will you push it under the door?' Petra made a huge effort and smiled at Manda. 'I'm not being rude. I just want a really early night.'

'OK. I'll not disturb you. Take care of yourself.'

Petra couldn't even be bothered to get any food for herself. She wanted someone to take care of her, without questions, without accusations. The thought of Christmas with her parents was like a faint glimmer of light at the end of the present dark tunnel.

Granville Antiques was very festive after the close of trading on the Saturday before Christmas. There was a huge gold- and silver-trimmed tree in the corner of the main display room, and every one of the shop's valuable Georgian candlesticks held a glowing red candle.

Hugo's staff moved around with drinks and canapés from guest to guest. There were enough people there to make the shop seem crowded, and Petra was able to lose herself among them without coming close to Hugo until just before she was thinking of leaving. It was sheer bad luck that made him change direction so that they came face to face in the angle of the staircase.

'What are you doing for Christmas, Petra?' he asked her, his tone politely social.

'Going home to Liverpool. And looking forward to it. I suppose you'll be having a quiet time with Alexander and your mother away?'

'It's not going to be quiet for long. I've three lots of workmen moving into different premises the day after Boxing Day.'

His using of his son as a weapon against her still rankled.

'What a good job you got Alexander out of the way, then,' she said, sipping her drink.

He looked hard at her. 'You could have phrased that more pleasantly. I didn't send him away for my own convenience. The paediatrician recommended a week or two somewhere warm, and I naturally followed his advice. Why not find out the facts before you put the wrong interpretation on events?'

'I didn't say any such thing.'

'Don't hedge. You certainly thought it.'

'Hugo,' she said tiredly, 'we've done this bit many times before. Can't we meet for once without arguing?'

'It doesn't seem like it, does it?' he said grimly. 'However, I'll try again. Your lease has only four more weeks to run after Christmas. Have you any idea what you'll do next?'

'No. I suppose you can't wait to gloat over getting rid of me.' She bit her lip. 'Sorry. My fault that time.'

He smiled, a smile that twisted her heart. 'Funnily enough, despite everything, it's going to be just a little bit dull without your brand of fireworks around.'

'Now I know it's Christmas. You're almost being civil to me.'

He raised his glass. 'Let's not push our luck. Better to end on that note. Happy Christmas, Petra.'

She raised her glass to his, carefully, because they were fine Victorian crystal. 'Happy Christmas.'

He moved on to speak to the man from the bookshop, and Petra found a resting place for her glass and quietly left.

\*     \*     \*

When she awoke on Sunday morning, it soon became obvious that she was not well. A Christmas cold, she thought glumly. Just her luck.

There was a lot of washing and ironing and neglected cleaning to do before she left for Liverpool next day, and she struggled through it, telling herself that a cold was a cold and not to be given in to. However, by mid-afternoon she couldn't pretend any longer that she was just developing a minor ailment. She was alternately hot and cold, aching in every joint with a head to match, and she had stayed on her feet as long as she could without collapsing. She dosed herself with aspirin and took a hot-water bottle to bed.

After a night of tossing and turning and burning up with fever, she felt no better in the morning of Christmas Eve. Invalid tears stung her burning eyes. She wasn't going to be able to go home for Christmas. She couldn't bear the thought of even dressing, let alone attempting a journey at the wheel of a lethal weapon—and in any case, what was the point of inflicting a similar dose of flu on her parents?

Petra dragged herself to the phone, reassured her mother quite falsely as to there being someone else in the house, and food in her larder, and staggered back to bed feeling as weak as one of the kittens Manda and Joe had gone off with.

It had been snowing all night, and the lane in front of the house was filling up between its banks with an unmarked carpet of white that somehow emphasised most cruelly her isolation.

The house had never felt so empty, with no friendly noises from the other floors. The milk was cancelled, there was no more fuel indoors for the solid-fuel stove, and the thought of going out through a foot of snow to refill the bucket was both unbearable and impossible.

Petra filled the hot-water bottle again, a few self-pitying tears sliding down her cheeks as she did so, and buried herself under the duvet again, angry with her own weakness, with life in general, and with whoever had infected her with these sickening flu germs in particular.

She must have dozed for quite a time because it was growing dusk when the telephone roused her. She staggered out of bed, hugging her dressing-gown round her shoulders, and croaked a feeble, 'Hello?' into it.

'Petra?' The voice was male and very surprised. She was too befuddled to recognise it, just as she had been quite unable to remember her own phone number when she picked up the phone.

'Yes.' Who was it?

'Not gone yet? You're going to be driving in the dark to Liverpool. Is that wise?' Hugo. The very last person to be of any use to her.

'I'm not going,' she said tersely.

'You sound . . .' His voice sharpened. 'Why aren't you going? Are you ill?'

'I've got flu. What do you want, Hugo? I don't feel like talking.'

'Is someone with you?'

'I don't normally throw parties when I'm ill.'

'There's no one else in the house at all?'

'No. And I wouldn't want to talk to them either if they were,' she said, and slammed the phone down.

Why couldn't it have been someone she could have asked to come over and bring her a miracle cure? But, even if it had been a more possible caller, nobody would get down Hob Lane until it was cleared or cleared itself. She knew that from her aunt's accounts of previous snowed-in winters.

She burrowed under the duvet again. Her head was pounding, and she wondered weakly whether she could take any more aspirins. When had she had the last? She couldn't even remember that. Sleep saved her any further wonderings.

It was fully dark now, and somebody was knocking on her bedroom window. Petra sat up, clutching the duvet, fear added to her other symptoms. She was in no state to deal with an intruder.

But intruders didn't hammer on the window to advertise their presence, did they? Nor did they shout your name.

'Petra! Petra! Are you all right?'

It was Hugo again, and in person this time. The last person she wanted to see or to see her, with her hair damp from fever, her nose pink and shining, and her eyes feeling as though they had been sandpapered.

'Petra!' he called again. 'I know you're there.'

'Of course I'm damned well here!' she croaked angrily. 'Please go away.'

'Just open the door and let me in—and that's the last thing you'll have to do, I promise.'

She struggled into her old red dressing-gown. 'It's the last thing I'll be alive to do, probably,' she said ungraciously as she went to open the door.

He was well wrapped up against the weather in a navy-blue duffel coat, red scarf and boots, and his hair was powdered with snow. He brought a blast of ice-cold air into the house with him.

'How did you get here?' Petra asked, shivering. 'The lane doesn't look passable—at least, it didn't earlier on, and it's been snowing ever since.'

He was stripping off his bad-weather gear. 'The main road's not too bad—not wonderful, but still just about usable. I left the car in the lay-by there and walked down the lane.'

He reached out and put a hand on her forehead. His hand was blissfully cool. 'You're burning up, aren't you?' His voice was sympathetic and she couldn't cope with sympathy.

'And I look a fright, and feel ten times as bad as I look.' A couple of tears spilled down her cheeks. 'And I never cry!' she said furiously. 'What on earth is the matter with me?'

He put an arm round her shoulder and propelled her back from the communal hall into her own flat.

'You're over-tired. You're disappointed about Christmas, and you're ill. Isn't that enough reason?' He looked round. 'Why is it so cold in here?'

She gestured towards the dark, cheerless doors of the solid-fuel stove. 'I couldn't face going out for fuel. The store's behind a snowdrift round the back of the house.'

'Haven't you got an electric fire?'

She had been too stupefied to think of it. 'Yes. Behind the sofa.'

He brought the fire round and plugged it in in front of the sofa, then disappeared into the bedroom, which he found by some kind of remote radar, coming back with the hot-water bottle under his arm, and the blanket she had piled on top of her duvet, which he tucked round her.

'Now—if you can bear to sit there for a little while, I'm going to change your bed.'

She groaned at the thought of the unfresh, fever-damp bedclothes.

'*Please* don't.'

'Don't be so ridiculous,' he chided, then continued, 'And then I'm going to fill your hot-water bottle. After which I'll see to the stove and get the central heating going and bring in the stuff I've brought. By then your

bed should be warm and comfortable enough for you to
get back into it.'

'What stuff?' she asked hazily. 'Why are you here?
Why are you doing this?'

He knuckled her cheek gently. 'Don't ask stupid questions. You *need* somebody, don't you? Does it really
matter who it is? If it makes you feel any better, you
can regard it as an afterthought of a move in the tit-for-
tat business. Something to balance what you did for
Alexander.'

Her eyes pricked again. She buried her face in the
blanket. 'For heaven's sake, don't be nice to me. It's like
turning on a tap.'

'Just shut up and get warm, then.'

He made off for the bedroom and there were
businesslike sounds of activity coming through the open
door for a time. Petra snuggled down in the blanket's
warmth, her protruding toes curling with appreciation
of the heat from the fire.

She watched Hugo come and go in sleepy silence, and,
apart from the odd shrewd, assessing look, he let her
be. Then he disappeared and she heard him carrying what
sounded like an incredible amount of things into the
kitchen—at least four trips out to the front of the house.

When he came back into the sitting-room with a bucket
of fuel, she looked up at him. 'What on earth have you
been doing?'

'Unloading the sledge.'

'*Sledge*?'

'Yes. Alexander's sledge. With the amount of snow
there's been, it was the best way I could think of to move
the turkey and the rest down from the car.'

'*Turkey*?' She seemed to be reduced to one-word
questions.

He grinned at her. 'Come on. Don't tax your brain too much. The bed should be nice and warm now.' Without waiting for an answer, he scooped her up, blanket and all, and carried her through into the bedroom, where he not only tucked her into a blissfully warm and fresh bed, but brought her a flannel to wipe her face and went so far as to brush back her hair himself.

Petra closed her eyes and lay thankfully back on the pillows.

'I—I'm glad you're here,' she said huskily.

'Must be a very high fever,' he said sceptically, taking the flannel and towel back into the bathroom across the lobby.

'Hugo,' she said drowsily. 'Why did you bring a turkey?'

'We shall need it tomorrow.'

'We? Tomorrow?' She was back in the one-word-question mode.

'You don't think I'd walk out on anyone in your state, do you? Drink this. It's one of those drinks with honey and lemon. Then you're going to sleep, and when you've had a sleep you'll have some soup to set you up for the night. When did you last eat?'

'I can't remember. I haven't wanted to.'

'And, judging by the look of your refrigerator, you couldn't have done much about it if you *had* wanted to.'

'I was going away, wasn't I?'

'And now you're staying put and being looked after.'

The last hazy thing she remembered before sinking into sleep again was his face as he turned back in the bedroom doorway, and said, his voice gentle after the bracing teasing tone he had adopted since he arrived, 'No one should be alone at Christmas. Especially someone like you.'

After her soup—home-made chicken broth, which she drank ravenously in spite of all her protestations—and another round of lemon and honey, this time with a measure of whisky mixed in, she settled down and prepared to sleep again.

What was it he had said after the bit about nobody should spend Christmas alone? 'Especially someone like you.' *No*. She had got to have imagined that. He only used that particular phrase in the context of unpleasant matters. She was more feverish than she had thought.

She slept again, this time the night through.

'How are you this morning?' Hugo asked, coming into her room with a cup of tea at nine o'clock on Christmas morning. 'Much better, judging by the look of you.'

Petra was almost clear-eyed again. It must have been a strong but short-lived set of germs. She saw that Hugo was already dressed in jeans and a light green sweater that made his eyes look very green to match.

'Thanks,' she said, taking the tea. 'Yes, I feel much better this morning. Where did you sleep?'

'On your sofa. You might look out for a longer one if you're going to get yourself into any more emergency situations.'

'Sorry about that. Happy Christmas, anyway.'

He smiled. 'Happy Christmas.'

Petra sipped her tea. 'You must go home now, Hugo.'

'No chance, I'm afraid. My turkey's already sizzling away in your oven.'

'But what if Alexander and your mother ring Abbotswood? They're sure to do that on Christmas Day. They'll be frightfully worried.'

'No, they won't. I've arranged to call them today at lunchtime. I can do that from here. I'll have the call metered, of course.'

Petra drew herself up. 'Don't be so absurd. You deserve more than a measly call to Alexander. Try to pay for it and I'll throw you out.'

He looked at her pale face and dark-shadowed eyes. 'You and whose army? You don't look fit to throw a turkey drumstick out.'

'I shall look better when I'm up and dressed.'

'"Up" means as far as the sofa in front of the fire. That's a statement, not a question. But if you feel equal to a bath when you've had the fruit juice and toast I'm going to bring you, fair enough. Like some coffee with it?'

Petra sank back on the pillows. 'You're an incredibly bossy person. Yes, please.'

He grinned at her. 'Breakfast coming up, then.'

She was, in fact, glad to limit dressing to pulling on a blue tracksuit once she had had her bath, and even more glad to flop on the sofa with a blanket and pillows.

'Does being under the weather incline you towards twentieth-century clothes?' Hugo asked on seeing the tracksuit.

'I'm always willing to consider all styles,' she told him.

There were delicious smells coming from the kitchen, carols playing softly on the radio, and a traditional white world framed in the window. The house that had seemed so cold and isolated and lonely yesterday was a warm, glowing jewel of a place today.

Petra's mother, who called late morning, was reassured by the background noises she could hear down the phone.

'It sounds as though your friends are looking after you well,' she commented.

'They are. Extremely well,' Petra said, her eyes following Hugo's movements as she spoke.

'What a good job someone was around. Any chance of your making a late trip up here?'

'Maybe.' Petra felt strangely reluctant to think of being anywhere but here, and now. 'I've still got cotton-wool legs today, but the shop's closed all week, so there's plenty of time.'

'Good. Dad and I want very much to see you, of course. Give my love and thanks to your friends, darling.'

Petra edited the message. 'My mother sends her thanks for looking after me.' She looked at him. 'That goes for me, too. I can't get over how strangely nice you're being.'

'A backhander of a compliment, if I ever heard one. Put my niceness down to a Christmas miracle. You know Hardy's poem about the animals being given the gift of speech at midnight on Christmas Eve? Perhaps I have miraculously been given a short-lived spell of charm. Make the most of it.'

'Oh, believe me, I am,' Petra said, snuggling back against the pillows.

Christmas Day passed as all Christmas Days had a habit of doing. A long, delicious, amazingly well-cooked meal. The Queen's speech. Tea. The decision that no further food could be faced that day, broken mid-evening by enthusiastic tackling of cold ham and salad. Talk and television, and later still a game of Scrabble in front of the glowing stove. Petra conceded victory to Hugo and smothered a yawn, slumping back on the sofa.

'Tired?' he asked. 'Time for a last whisky, honey and lemon perhaps.'

'I don't really think it's necessary now. I've been feeling better and better all day.'

'I should have one. Make sure of a good night's sleep.' He got up and went off to the kitchen. Petra sat gazing dreamily into the heart of the stove.

He came back and gave her her drink, then sat down at her side, long legs stretched out towards the fire. Petra sipped her hot drink and ended up feeling pleasantly light-headed.

'This has been the most unexpected Christmas Day ever. But I've really enjoyed it,' she told Hugo, meaning it.

He turned his head to look at her. 'So have I.'

All day her indisposition had been enough to blunt Petra to the fact that it was Hugo Baron here with her, doing such incredible things as cooking in her kitchen, moving around her flat with as much familiarity as if he owned it.

But that simple exchange of words, and the meeting of their eyes as the words were spoken, seemed to take the mood of the evening and transform it into something else, something dangerous. Something was waiting to happen...words were waiting to be spoken. But neither happening nor words were wanted, she knew. As sure as night followed day, they would be regretted by one or the other of them.

She edged sharply forward and stood up. 'I shall go to my parents' tomorrow,' she said decisively. 'I shall be perfectly fit to travel by then.'

Hugo stood. 'And I shall collect my things together and go back to Abbotswood now, since my presence here is no longer necessary. Don't bother to hang around. Get off to bed before the effect of your drink wears off. I'll clear up and let myself out.'

She lingered, aimlessly watching as he gathered up glasses and plates and took them out to the kitchen. She resented his busyness. It excluded her.

'Well—go on!' he said briskly, coming back and looking round the room. 'You're doing no good here.'

'Will you be all right—going back through the snow?'

He gave her an exasperated look. 'I got here, didn't
I?'

'Yes. But I didn't know about that. Now I shall be
wondering. You could let me know you're not stuck in
a snowdrift between here and Whittington. Just a quick
call.'

'Oh, for heaven's sake!' he said impatiently. Then,
when she still hovered in the bedroom doorway, 'I'll dial
your number and let the phone ring three times. You
needn't get out of bed to pick it up. No one else is likely
to phone you at this time, I imagine, so that should tell
you what you want to know. Satisfied?'

She gave him a baleful look. 'It's worn off, hasn't it?'

He looked blankly at her. 'What are you talking
about?'

'The charm.'

'Christmas doesn't last forever,' he said shortly, and
shut himself in the kitchen.

Petra withdrew to her own shut-away area of bedroom
and bathroom. She had been amazingly contented all
day. Now everything had gone flat and she was very tired
indeed. She filled her hot-water bottle from the tap,
feeling stupidly peeved that it hadn't been filled for her,
which was quite ridiculous since she had been pro-
claiming her own recovery all day.

She lay in bed, listening to the muffled noises from
the kitchen. In a little while she heard the closing of the
flat door, and a few moments later the closing of the
heavy front door of the house.

She came amazingly close to tears again. He had not
even shouted goodnight to her. He could have done that
at least, after today. It seemed impossible that, after the
warmth and rightness of Christmas Day, yet again they
should have parted on the note they had.

'Christmas doesn't last forever,' he had said. But she had an awful feeling that as far as she was concerned the effect of this Christmas Day would not be easily forgotten.

You *can't*, she told herself, thrashing over angrily in her bed, you can't *possibly* feel the way you do. He's someone who has told you quite definitely that you're the last person in the world he wants to get involved with. Isn't that enough to stop you mooning about him like this?

Apparently it was not. When the phone rang, she shot out of bed and ran through to the sitting-room. One ring more than the three he had promised, and she would snatch up the phone and he would be telling her that he couldn't think why he had left as he had—why he had left at all. Her hand hovered eagerly over the phone.

Three rings, and no more. Hugo Baron was a man who meant what he said. Anything else came from her imagination. More fool her.

She trailed back to bed. Tomorrow she would go to Liverpool. When she came back, she would have recovered her sanity. And it wouldn't be long until the end of January.

# CHAPTER NINE

COMING back from Liverpool full of good resolutions, Petra turned into the Oak House drive only to find how shallow was her new-found resolve to stop entertaining impossible ideas about Hugo Baron.

His car was in her drive. Her return had coincided exactly, thanks to a side-swipe from fate, with Hugo's delivery of flowers to Manda, presumably as a thank-you for Alexander's kitten. Manda, with misguided tact, withdrew hurriedly indoors, and Hugo came over to the car as Petra was getting out.

She might never have resolved anything. Her heart did a savage series of aerobics in her chest, and words deserted her.

'Hello, Petra,' Hugo said calmly. 'Did you have a good trip to Liverpool?'

'Lovely, thanks.' It was only half a truth. It had, as always, been lovely to warm herself in the glow of her parents' affection, but there had been so much this time that she couldn't bring herself to say to them. And this man, who was capable of having such an effect on her while looking so damned cool and remote himself, was responsible for that.

'And are you fully recovered now?'

'Perfectly.' But don't ask that question about anything but the common cold... she thought. Ask me if I'm over thinking about you, and I'll most likely fling myself against that Pringle sweater of yours and do my damnedest to shrink it.

'Good. I won't keep you standing out here, then.' He
nodded a quick goodbye, then added as a courteous afterthought, 'Want any help with luggage?'

'No, thanks, this is all I have,' Petra said hurriedly,
grabbing her holdall from the back seat.

He took her at her word and left.

Petra let herself in to what she expected would be an
ice-cold flat, and found it warm and cosy with the solid-
fuel stove glowing red. Manda came hurrying down to
say hello, and told her that Hugo was responsible for
her comfort.

'He came round this morning to ask when you'd be
back and tell us you'd been ill, then when we said you'd
phoned to say you'd be back late today he borrowed
your key to light the fire and get the place warm for you.
Insisted on doing it himself. He came back this afternoon
and stoked up again, though I'd said that Joe would do
it, and at the same time he gave me flowers because of
the kitten.' She looked at Petra, head on one side, a
thoughtful look in her eyes. 'He's not at all like we first
thought him to be, is he?'

When Manda had gone back upstairs, Petra sat in
front of the stove, staring into its glowing heart, and
shed a miserable tear or two.

It wasn't fair that Hugo should care about her welfare,
and yet make it so clear that he couldn't, wouldn't, didn't
care *for* her. No love should mean no kindness. Kindness
of this type hurt rather than helped.

She jumped to her feet angrily. 'You make me sick,'
she told herself. 'This will not do, Petra Collins. Snap
out of it.'

The phone rang later that evening. A man she knew
socially was keen to take her to a New Year's Eve ball
at a plushy hotel in town. It was a last-minute invitation

because he had been let down by his original partner, he told her with embarrassed honesty.

It could have been more flatteringly put, but it was an invitation, and she needed to fill her calendar with anything that would make her less liable to relapse on the Hugo front. And Paul Webster was pleasant enough company.

'That's all right, Paul,' Petra said. 'As a matter of fact, I haven't made any plans for New Year's Eve, and I'm rather regretting it—so I'd love to go.'

'You would? Great!' They discussed times and arrangements, and Petra sat on after she had put the phone down, thinking how little the idea of going to a ball with anyone really appealed to her at the moment, despite her pretence at enthusiasm. The sooner she was back at work, the better, really. Holidays left far too much time for the wrong kind of thoughts to multiply like yeast in the mind.

She had a lovely evening dress that she had been waiting for a suitable occasion to wear. It dated from the twenties, with all the easy, deceptive simplicity of line of the clothes of the period. The slender, low-waisted tunic top was of pale grey silk voile encrusted with a swirling pattern of tiny crystals. The handkerchief-point skirt had a crystal motif on the point of every floating panel. Along the shoulder-line and down through the elbow-length sleeves *diamanté* buttons marked the meeting-point of each open scallop. It was a dream of a dress, and Petra would have preferred to wear it for a dream of a person, but Paul Webster would have to do.

She drew the line at a true twenties hairstyle to match the dress. That would have meant cropping her long hair. But she compromised by having it done, at daunting cost, in a complicated nape-of-the-neck swirl that gave a

suitable neat shape, and made a further concession to
the twenties by tying a pearl-grey ribbon round her
forehead. Crystal drop-earrings completed the picture.

She looked good, but without sparkle, she thought.
A bit pale, a bit peaky, as Manda was fond of saying.
Still, definitely not, on the surface at least, like someone
whose world felt to be falling apart. So she was
reasonably proud of herself.

'Who was it who let you down at the last minute,
then?' she asked Paul as they walked through the carpeted entrance of the hotel where the ball was being held.

'I'm not sure that we should be holding this conversation. It's rather indelicate, don't you think?' he said,
his nice face caught halfway between rueful amusement
and embarrassment.

'Whyever not? I know something happened to change
your plans, and I don't in the least mind talking about
it.' Who knew? It might even take her mind off her own
troubles.

'In that case, if you really want to know, it was a last-
minute difference of opinion.'

'With?' Petra prompted.

'Joanne Morton. Do you know her?'

'No, I don't think so.'

'She's one of the hunting set.'

'Then I certainly wouldn't know her. Not my scene,'
Petra said decisively.

Paul pulled a wry 'me too' face. 'That was what the
difference of opinion was about. I can't stand the idea
of hunting. She was brought up to regard it as a routine
part of life. Why on earth I had to get involved with
someone with such opposing views to my own, I can't
imagine. But you can't always choose the person you're
going to find yourself attracted to, can you?'

'You certainly can't,' Petra said quietly.

They went into the ballroom and chose a table.

'The problem arose,' Paul said, going back to the subject of Joanne, who might be out of sight but was certainly not out of mind, 'because I wanted her to go to a Boxing Day lunch party with me. She said she always went to the Meet that day—had done ever since she was a child. I told her she should have managed to do some growing up since those days, and before we knew it there was a full-scale row in progress, ending with Joanne saying we might as well part right there and then, and save ourselves a load of trouble. I told her it suited me very well, and that was that. So there you have it—the sorry story of why I was left with two tickets for a ball and no girl to come with me. I'm glad you were free. It would have been a miserable New Year's Eve otherwise.'

'Pretty uneventful for me, too. Anyway, since we're here, let's dance,' Petra said with determination, and they joined the swirling crowds on the floor.

Paul was a reasonable dancer, and pleasant enough company when not brooding about his ill-fated love-life. A tolerable half-hour passed, and then, as they were dancing a slow waltz, Petra felt him tense and looked up.

'She's here. Joanne. It never occurred to me that she'd find another partner,' he said.

Petra studied his face. 'Is this going to be awkward?'

He relaxed slightly. 'Why should it be? We're both free agents.' He demonstrated his freedom by holding Petra more closely and taking advantage of a bit of floor space to spin her round.

'What is she wearing?' Petra asked with interest.

'Red. Wouldn't you know it? Only of course the in-crowd call it pink. Short hair. Dark. Opposite us now.'

There was only one girl who fitted the description. The sight of her made Petra draw in her breath sharply.

The girl was dancing, quite unaware of her observers, in the arms of Hugo Baron. His eyes met Petra's, froze and held hers for a moment, then he gave a brief nod before disappearing from view in the press of dancers.

'Has she seen me?' Paul asked, studiously not looking across the ballroom.

'I don't think so.' Petra had never imagined that Hugo would be here. The situation was almost farcical. She must concentrate on that side of it. 'As a matter of fact,' she told Paul, 'your Joanne is dancing with my present landlord, with whom I don't exactly see eye to eye.'

'Oh, great! This evening has enormous potential,' he said gloomily.

They sat the next dance out, and saw the girl in the red dress dancing with someone else.

'Another of the huntin', shootin' and fishin' brigade,' Paul said scathingly. A shadow fell on their table, and Petra looked up to see Hugo standing there.

'Good evening, Petra,' he said.

She had been prepared to speak to him at some point in the evening, but even so it was hard to give the impression of being calm.

'Good evening, Hugo. Do you know Paul Webster?'

'We haven't met.' The two men shook hands, Paul grim-faced.

'You don't mind if I steal your partner for this dance, do you?' Hugo asked urbanely.

'I was expecting it,' Paul said ungraciously.

Hugo slid Petra's chair back as she rose, not responding to the hostility in Paul's voice. But once they were on the floor he remarked, 'You seem to have got yourself a rather surly partner.'

'Paul's a sweetie!' she over-enthused.

He looked down at her, poker-faced. 'And how well do you know this "sweetie" of a man?'

'I've known him for ages.'

'I didn't ask how long, I asked how well.'

'Well enough to come to a dance with him,' she said crisply.

'But not well enough to send an SOS for him to look after you when you're ill.'

'I didn't *ask* anybody to look after me, Hugo,' she emphasised. 'And, to be blunt, is how well I know Paul any business of yours?'

'You're right. Absolutely no business at all.' They danced in a prickly silence for a few moments. It hadn't taken long to get to that stage.

'I hadn't expected to see you here,' he said at length.

'It was a last-minute decision.'

'For me too. I came along to make the numbers even in the party I'm with. How did your last-minute decision come about?'

'I see no point in going into that,' Petra replied, rather tired of the Paul and Joanne saga. 'We're here, and that's that.'

'I was under the impression that I was making conversation.'

'If you have to "make conversation", why bother to ask me to dance?'

He looked down at her. 'For someone who looks like an angel, you certainly have a devil's tongue.'

She glared back at him, hackles rising, then, as he raised his eyebrows, his expression softened by a trace of humour, she relaxed.

'Oh—there we go again!'

'Let's impose a ban on conversation,' he suggested. 'The dancing's all right.'

The dancing was very all right. It was only too easy to feel that she was at one with this man when they danced together. The knowledge that they were in every

other respect poles apart made the physical harmony between them all the more poignant, though. Better by far
not to be in this situation. Fate was unnecessarily cruel
to have brought them together, and with the double link
of connected partners.

The music stopped. Petra turned back to her table,
with a quick, 'Thanks, Hugo.' But then she stopped.
'Oh, dear! I don't somehow think that Paul wants me
back there at the moment,' she said.

The girl in the red dress, Hugo's partner, was carrying
on a spirited conversation with Paul, gesticulating and
tossing her head.

'What goes on?' Hugo asked.

'Can't you guess? My partner was your partner's
abortive partner-to-be.'

He gave a low laugh. 'How ironic. We'd better do the
charitable thing and make ourselves scarce so that they
can iron out their differences, don't you think? I'll get
drinks and we'll take them out into the conservatory.'

Petra resigned herself to further ordeal by Hugo. It
was quiet in the conservatory while she waited for him
to come back with the drinks, only the delicate sound
of a fountain and the muted voices of another party at
the far end of the leafy, lamplit room breaking the
silence.

Hugo returned, sitting beside her on the wicker couch,
and Petra wished she had taken a chair, as anyone with
half a brain would have done.

'Is Alexander home yet?' she asked, and at once their
previous discussion about Alexander's attachment to her
was there, waving red flags in her mind.

'Not yet,' he said coldly, betraying the fact that he
too remembered. 'They'll be back just before school
starts again.'

The fountain played on. The other party drifted past, on their way back into the ballroom.

'Have you any plans for the end of January?' he asked.

Because it was painful to think of the end of the month and the end of her time in Granville Row, Petra answered with reckless imagination.

'Several. I may let my flat and go to London for a while. Three rents would subsidise me very well, and Camden Market could be interesting through the spring and summer. Or I may even go abroad. My kind of bits and pieces should sell well on the Continent. America would be a good place, too.' She was warming to her theme. 'They like things from the old country, I'm told. Though there'd be more trouble getting things over there. Not as easy as nipping to and fro across the Channel.'

'In other words, the world's your oyster. How unbearably old you make me feel. Are you sure you couldn't fit in the Hippy Trail as well?'

She looked stonily at him. 'There's nothing hippy about me.'

'Just a spirited readiness for adventure. A constant willingness to up and go.'

'Like your late wife. I'll save you the trouble of saying it.' They glared at each other, and Petra put down her glass. 'I think it's time for me to up and go now. There's no point in sitting here exchanging insults. I can do without that.'

She stood, and Hugo unfolded his long length and rose with her. 'Petra——'

She turned and made the mistake of looking into his eyes—green, not grey, she realised, and looking at her with concern that made her legs go weak.

'Don't do anything foolish when you leave Cheltenham, will you?'

'Of course not.'

Silence fell again while they went on looking at each other, so close, and yet so far from each other. Hugo moved a little nearer, and the tension between them became unbearable.

'I expect those two will have sorted something out by now,' Petra said with an effort. 'Let's go and find out.'

Something had certainly been sorted out. Paul and Joanne were dancing, with not a scrap of room for the proverbial pin between them. Joanne's head was on Paul's shoulder, his face pressed against her hair, his arms round her, hands resting possessively on her hips, hers clasped round his neck.

'I begin to feel a little superfluous,' Hugo said.

'I'm getting the same message. I doubt whether they even remember that they came with someone else.'

Hugo turned resignedly to face her. 'I'm quite prepared to partner you for the rest of the evening.'

'Quite prepared.' It could hardly have sounded less enthusiastic.

'Thanks,' she said quietly, 'but I don't think either of us would benefit from that.'

'As you wish,' he replied stiffly.

'I shall go home—rather thankfully. I've got a headache.'

'Perhaps the ribbon round your forehead is responsible.'

'And perhaps something quite different is to blame,' she said with a dark look.

'I was going to add "charming though it looks". You must let me run you home if you insist on going.'

'No.' She spoke with rude abruptness. 'Sorry to be so emphatic, but I don't think it would improve my headache. I really do have one, and since we seem incapable of ordinary small talk I'd sooner take a taxi.'

'Then I shall call one for you.'

She watched him walk away, tall, unbearably handsome in his evening suit, and she ached at the things they did to each other. Why should it be like this? In books it was a case of happy ever after. Wedding bells and confetti. Her own ever after stretched ahead, appallingly bleak.

Hugo came back while she was collecting her cloak.

'Two minutes. They seem to be at a loose end just now.'

'If you speak to Paul, tell him I'll phone him tomorrow,' she said as they walked towards the door.

'I should think he'll not only phone you but send you an enormous bouquet,' Hugo said disapprovingly.

'It doesn't matter in the least to me,' she told him with absolute honesty.

'Nothing does, really, does it?'

If she had thought about that, she might have disgraced herself by bursting into tears. She buried the words and refused to consider them.

'I hope you won't behave unpleasantly towards them. I think they really do care for each other,' she warned.

'More fool them for behaving in such an idiotic way, then. But you needn't worry. I have no intention of making a scene. There are plenty of other partners, and I pride myself that my manners are adequate.'

He spoke to the taxi driver, giving him her address, and closed the cab door on her with a quiet, 'Goodnight.'

When Petra tried to pay the driver back in Hob Lane, he waved aside her note. 'That's taken care of, miss. The gentleman saw to it before we left.'

Petra let herself into her house, and leaned against the front door in the darkness.

'Damn him!' she said through clenched teeth. 'Damn him for being what he is.' Quarrelsome and yet correct. Insulting, but generous. Cruel as well as kind.

Reasonable one minute, irrational the next. All those conflicting things, and one thing more. Unforgettable too, she was very much afraid.

Alexander called in at the shop on his first day back at school. He was wearing new uniform, a little long in the sleeve and trouser leg. It made him look vulnerable, and Petra longed to hug him. He was honey-brown from his weeks in the Bahamas.

'You've grown a lot,' Petra told him.

'I know. I'm as big as Nigel Forest now. That should stop him bossing around. He's as jealous as anything about the kitten.' His face went serious. 'Is Ockie sad, Petra?'

'Because of the kitten going away?'

'Yes. It is sad when people go away, isn't it?'

'I think cats are a bit different from people, Alexander.'

That, it appeared, was the wrong thing to say. He kicked the carpet in silence for a moment, then looked up at her.

'You're going away, aren't you?'

'Yes, but I've got a house here, don't forget. I expect I'll be back from time to time,' she said briskly.

He seemed reassured and changed the subject, his forehead wrinkling in perfect imitation of Hugo's frown.

'Did you know that my *father* has got a *girlfriend*?' The use of the formal word, not Dad, and the emphasis given both words seemed to indicate that Alexander did not approve. Petra, though she despised herself for feeling that way, found the information upsetting too.

'Has he?' she said non-committally.

'Her mother's a friend of my grandma's, and they were at the airport when we came back from the Bahamas.

My father talked to her far more than he did to me. And they're going riding on Sunday afternoon.'

Petra made an attempt to think charitably of the event. 'Well, at least it's better than "stodging", isn't it?'

Alexander gave a bleak smile in acknowledgement of her use of his word.

'Grandma says it will be good for him. But I don't know. This girl—she's called Caroline—asked me if I would like to come too. She said she had a pony that would be just right for me.' He fiddled with the edge of a table. 'I don't much like horses, actually,' he added with studied casualness.

'Maybe you'll feel differently when you're bigger and horses seem smaller,' Petra told him diplomatically.

'Maybe.' He didn't sound convinced. 'Petra—why can't you come to the house again like you did before I went into hospital? I'm sure you'd be much gooder for my dad.'

'Better,' Petra corrected automatically. 'Well, Alexander, I don't think that's something you can arrange. You see, parents have a habit of choosing their own friends, not letting their children do it for them.'

'That's what my *father* said when I asked him the same thing.'

'There you are, then. It must be true.'

He kicked at the carpet, then remembered that he shouldn't.

'Sorry. I'd better go or I'll get into trouble.' He looked accusingly at Petra. 'Grown-ups are always bad-tempered after Christmas. At least, my dad is.'

'Go on, Alexander,' she said. 'Give your poor father a rest.'

'He's just had a rest. More than three weeks of it. My grandma says, "Much good it's done him."' He grinned wickedly and darted off.

Caroline... Petra brooded. Caroline who was a long-standing friend of the family, whose roots were safely in this place, who wouldn't be tempted to wander. Horse-loving Caroline. She gazed at her reflection in a carved oak-framed mirror and tossed back her head with a fair imitation of a whinny.

'What on earth are you doing?' Hugo said, coming silently through the door, which Alexander must have left not properly shut.

Petra went bright scarlet. 'It would take too long to explain,' she said. She hadn't seen Hugo since New Year's Eve, and she didn't feel better for seeing him now. 'What can I do for you?' she asked quickly.

'I've got the next tenant for this place with me next door. Would it be convenient for me to bring him round to have a quick look over the premises? He needs to check shelving and storage space.'

'Perfectly convenient,' Petra agreed. 'As you can see, people aren't exactly queuing to get in today.'

He thanked her perfunctorily and disappeared, to return in a few minutes with a tall, fair-haired man. By this time a customer had come in and was questioning Petra about the history of a little footstool with a tapestry top, so that she could do no more than nod and smile a greeting to the two men, who moved quietly around the shop, speaking in low voices. They looked in the kitchen and then disappeared upstairs.

By the time the customer left, Hugo was out on the pavement, seeing off his next tenant. He came back into Collections seconds later.

'Thank you. I hope we didn't prejudice a sale?'

'Not at all. And this place is yours, when all's said and done.'

He lingered, looking keenly at her. 'You've lost weight, and there wasn't much there to begin with. Are you eating sensibly?'

'Like a horse.' Horse was the wrong word to choose with its unfortunate connotations. She turned away and rearranged a shelf, quite unnecessarily.

He went on looking at her. 'Have you made your plans yet?'

'It's only a week since you asked me that,' she said impatiently.

'And it's only three weeks until you'll find yourself up the creek without a paddle if you don't get round to organising yourself,' he retorted smartly.

'I'm quite used to looking after myself. I've done it for years,' she told him. She gave him a glittering, totally false smile. 'Don't worry. Something will turn up. It always does.'

'Micawberish philosophy is all very well. But look what happened to Micawber,' Hugo said, and walked briskly out of the shop.

Joe, on the milk-bottle run, met Petra in the hall on Saturday night as she came in at eleven o'clock.

'Hello. Been out?' he asked.

'For a meal—with the couple who made me superfluous on New Year's Eve, if Manda told you about it.'

'She did. What a pair! Did they give you a good time tonight? They jolly well should have.'

'It was a lovely meal.' But being with two people who had sorted out their differences—heaven knew how; she certainly hadn't been foolish enough to ask—and who were so much in love that it shone from them, was the very last thing someone in her own unloved state really needed.

'Come on up and have a bedtime drink,' Joe said, picking up the vibes. 'We haven't seen you for ages for a good old natter. What have you been doing? Hibernating?'

'Something like that,' Petra said. 'All right, Joe. I'll come up. I might even borrow Ockie tonight, if she's going begging.'

Joe looked down at her with quiet kindliness. 'Like that, is it? Well, the other kitten's gone now, so Ockie can probably do with a bit of TLC too. Up we go.'

An hour later, as she was leaving the homely clutter of Joe and Manda's flat with Ockie in her arms, Petra took a decisive step.

'If you know anyone who'd like to rent my flat for six months, it's on offer from the end of the month,' she announced.

'You're going away? Where?' Manda asked, surprised.

'Anywhere. I've just got the old wanderlust again. London, I expect. Then wherever the fancy takes me. I'm not really a staying-put type.'

At least, that was what they told her about herself, she thought as she went downstairs. But, if it were true, why did the thought of another town, another flat, other people, seem so unattractive? However, it made sense, given the circumstances, didn't it? And she had made the intention public now. She would have to go ahead and do it.

It was at a house sale the following weekend that Petra saw the tiny silvered baby's shoe. Wrinkled and bent to fit the foot that had worn it all those years ago, it had an unmistakable, identifying hole in the toe.

Petra cradled it in her hand, her fingers running over the give-away flaw that no silvering process could disguise, her heart suddenly full at the thought of the small boy who had worn it so many years ago, and the mother who so wanted to have it returned to her. She put it among her purchases, and phoned Mrs Baron's flat from the shop that afternoon when Manda, who had been standing in, had left.

To her dismay, the voice that answered the phone was Hugo's.

'Oh—I was expecting to speak to Mrs Baron,' Petra said, disconcerted. 'I thought you were next door.'

'I don't spend every waking moment there. With other premises to keep an eye on, the shop has to run itself some of the time. And I do occasionally give myself time off. What can I do for you?'

'I have a little something for Mrs Baron. I was hoping to call in at her flat on my way home from work this evening.'

'She won't be here. I'm about to take her back to Abbotswood for the weekend. She would be glad to see you there, no doubt.'

'I wouldn't like to intrude on your weekend.'

'You mean you wouldn't want to risk seeing me,' he said in a low voice. 'If it helps your decision-making, I shall be out riding on Sunday afternoon.'

Caroline again, Petra thought crossly. Two Sundays running. Caroline was obviously making the grade. She heard Mrs Baron speak, then take the phone from Hugo.

'Petra—I should love to see you before you move away. Do come over to Abbotswood on Sunday, and we'll have a nice, peaceful cup of tea together.'

It was impossible to refuse. 'If you're sure that isn't a nuisance,' Petra said doubtfully.

'Of course it isn't. Don't take any notice of Hugo. You know what he's like. I'll expect you around three, shall I?'

Petra wished she had never found the wretched shoe. More than that, she wished Mrs Baron had never arranged the problematic lease for the Granville Row shop. But the woman had meant to be kind. She wasn't to know what a Pandora's box it would open in Petra's life.

There was no mistaking the joy the shoe brought to Mrs Baron. She assured Petra that, although no gift had been necessary, none could have brought her more pleasure.

Hugo, true to his word, was away riding with Caroline, and Alexander was over at Nigel Forest's house for the afternoon—they were great friends now, apparently. So the afternoon was, as Mrs Baron had promised, nice and peaceful. Petra stayed for an hour, then, assuring Mrs Baron that she could perfectly well let herself out, she said her goodbyes and thanks, and went out to the van.

Hugo was leaning against it, his thick brown sweater, riding breeches and leather boots proof that he had been riding. But not long enough.

'I didn't expect to see you,' Petra said.

'I bet you didn't.' His mouth twisted ironically. 'But I meant to see you. I came back early. I've been waiting here for the past quarter of an hour.'

'There was nothing to prevent your coming in. I would have left earlier.'

'It's you I want to see; that's why I came back early. But I wasn't going to come into the house and give my dear, delightful mother the chance to add her six pennorth to what I have to say.'

'I can't think what you can possibly have to say,' Petra said discouragingly.

He took her arm. 'Come down the garden a little way and find out.'

She gave him a rather worried look, but his grip was firm and they were already moving along the path through the shrubbery and beyond the frozen fountain. She shivered a little.

'I won't keep you long,' he said as he stopped and faced her. 'Petra—I'm worried about you.'

'You have no need to be,' she told him firmly.

'I think I have.' He paused, seeming strangely diffident about what he had it in mind to say. Petra felt correspondingly nervous too, without having the least idea why.

'I don't like the idea of your going away with no firm idea of what you are going to do with yourself. Anything could happen.'

'Really, Hugo!' she said impatiently. 'What I do is my business.'

'I would like to make it mine,' he said firmly, his words rocking her back on her heels. What was he saying? A wave of hot confusion ran through her in spite of the chill January wind blowing through the garden.

'There is something I want to ask you. An offer I want to make.' He looked away, seeming oddly uncertain of himself, then looked back at her. 'And I hope you will think hard about it before you answer.'

Petra felt that her heart was going to stop. Her eyes widened as she looked at him, trying desperately to read his intention.

'Will you stay on a little longer? Give yourself time to think sensibly about what you are going to do with your life? I can find work for you in Granville Antiques on three days of the week. One of my girls is getting married and would prefer to work part-time. You really could be quite useful to me.'

Petra came down to earth with a cruel thud. Work for him? Be 'quite useful' to him? That was the offer? With a superhuman effort she found her voice.

'Thank you, Hugo. I can see that you mean to be kind. But I must say straight away that nothing on earth would make me accept your offer.'

His eyes went steely grey. 'I asked you to think before answering.'

'I don't need to. You're the last person in the world I would ever work for.' Her indignation rose in her throat. 'As a matter of fact, I would rather die than work for you. So you can—you can stuff your three days a week!'

She ran away up the path and tumbled into the van. It started at the first attempt, and she was off down the drive before Hugo reached the top of the path.

Fool! she told herself painfully. Mad, unrealistic fool. For a brief moment back there she had thought she knew what Hugo Baron was leading up to. Not to the offer of a job. Not to the chance of being 'quite useful' to him. She had actually believed that the man was about to ask her to marry him. How could she have been such a self-deluding idiot?

It was long past the time that she should get right away from him and find her sanity again.

# CHAPTER TEN

THE last time she had been in Camden Market, Petra had found it full of heady excitement, a kaleidoscope of colour and sound. Today, there on a prospecting Sunday visit, it just seemed a crush and a cacophony. She hadn't been able to get away quickly enough.

She made excuses for herself. She had driven down from Cheltenham, and the M40 had been busy enough, but nothing in comparison with the London streets. That had depleted her energy before she started the search for accommodation. Where did all the people come from? Sunday was as busy and commercial as any other day.

The search for somewhere to live had been a depressing business. She hated the estate agents' double talk. Nothing meant what it seemed to mean. She had looked at flats which were no more than bed-sits, and cramped ones at that. She had seen a 'basement apartment of character'—the character being age, dampness and decrepitude. She had finally paid a staggeringly high month's rent in advance on a second-floor flat consisting of two small rooms and two cupboards—one of which served as kitchen, the other as shower and toilet. Decent enough, but with a view of nothing more inspiring than shabby roof-tops and acres of railway lines.

Now she was on her way back, the level Oxfordshire countryside giving way to the green hills of the Cotswolds. And she was thinking how crazy she was to be leaving Oak House with its lovely views of fields across Hob Lane for the kind of home she had secured for

herself, and to which she would be going in just over a
week's time.

Sums replaced thoughts of views. So far no one had
materialised as tenant for the ground floor of Oak
House. The two other rents would just about cover the
London flat. Hope Street was the address—a misnomer
if ever there was one. Other bills would have to come
out of her sales and her savings. But how on earth did
people manage who hadn't got a kindly Aunt Jess to
leave them property and subsidise their existence?

If the worst came to the worst, she could always come
back to rent-free Oak House. She frowned at the road
ahead. Come back and risk bumping into Hugo, hearing
about Hugo, reading, perhaps, of his marriage to horsy
Caroline? *No*. That was the whole reason for going away,
wasn't it? She would go away and stay away until Hugo
Baron's existence meant no more to her than that of the
rest of the world's population.

The last week at Collections had been surprisingly busy,
with friends and choir acquaintances coming into the
shop to say goodbye, and more often than not buying
something. Petra had arranged with Hugo that she would
drop the keys through the Granville Antiques door when
she had finished her packing up and cleaning on Sunday.

He had shaken hands with her and wished her good
luck. The next few seconds had been supremely difficult
as he kept hold of her hand and said almost diffidently,
'Petra—I hope things turn out well for you. You know
that, don't you?'

Ironic, that, coming from the man who could, if he
only knew it, fulfil all her needs and desires.

Now, on Sunday afternoon, with the light fading on
a cold, overcast day, she was packing her stock, surrounded by paper and boxes. She had been late getting

back after lunch—a farewell meal with Joe and Manda. There was still a lot to do, but she had refused their offer of help, knowing that she couldn't keep up the cheerfulness she had doggedly maintained throughout the meal.

She went upstairs to get the last of the things from up there, and when she came down Hugo was standing in the shop amid her chaos.

'I didn't hear you come in,' she said, not too cordially.

'You wouldn't have heard anyone come in. Thief, mugger, rapist—the door was unlocked, with free entry for all.' More gently he added, 'You really shouldn't be working in here alone at this time of day. It will be dark in a very short time.'

Petra indicated her stock. 'As you can see, there's plenty to do still. But you've made the point. I shall lock the door when you've gone.'

He nodded. 'Good.'

She looked at his riding gear and said stiffly, 'Have you had a good ride?'

'Very pleasant. The last of the snow is still on the hills, but the going's good.' He brought a sherry decanter from behind his back. 'I had to pick something up from the shop. I thought you might like to break for a farewell drink.'

'The glasses are packed,' she told him ungraciously.

The other hand appeared. 'I brought two of my own from next door.'

It was becoming more painful by the second to look at him. She was at the end of her tether as far as he was concerned. 'I really would rather not,' she told him. 'We had wine with lunch, and I don't think any more alcohol than I've already had with Joe and Manda would speed up the packing process at all.'

There was one brief second when she thought he was going to press on against her brusque refusal. But the next moment he was politely falling in with her wishes, saying calmly that he was sure she knew best about that, and he wouldn't delay her any longer.

'You're really on your way tomorrow, then?' he asked from the doorway.

'Yes.'

'Adventure round the corner?'

'I hope so.' She smiled brightly, feeling that her face would crack. Adventure round the corner? No. Just Hope Street, with its chimneys and railway lines.

He looked searchingly at her. 'You could change your mind, you know. The offer I made is still open.'

She shook her head. 'I'm not changing my mind.'

There was a silence.

'So all that remains is to wish you luck again.' He raised the decanter and glasses. 'I can't shake hands.'

'Let me open the door for you.' If he touched her, she felt that she would crumble into nothing at his feet.

'Don't forget to lock it.' He walked past her. Neither of them said goodbye.

She drew the bolts on both front and back doors, and then sat in the kitchen and wasted valuable time crying in the dark out there. Eventually, she told herself that that would definitely not do, and threw herself into the packing again with frenzied vigour, so much so that by the time the last box was filled she had the mother and father of all headaches.

She carried on until the last box was loaded into the van, then decided to give herself a break before tackling the final cleaning of the shop. There was a collection of empty bottles to be disposed of. A walk along to the bottle bank in the car park at the end of the road would perhaps clear her head. And a cup of tea when she got back would be welcome.

She filled the kettle and pushed aside a pile of unwanted packing paper to plug it in then flicked the switch. A flash and a fearsome crack made her jump back. So much for the cup of tea—but at least it was only the socket and kettle that were done for, not the lights as well. She left them on for when she got back, locked up the shop and set off along the road. Not being able to have a cup of tea was just one more bad thing in a bad day.

Once the bottles were disposed of, she wandered through from the car park into the adjoining park, which was deserted at this time of day, but bright and unghostly in the moonlight. She sat on a seat for a long time, drained of energy and utterly dejected, until at last she summoned up the will to walk on through the park and into the road at the far side, from which she could return by a circular route to the shop.

When she turned back into Granville Row at the top end, Petra was stopped dead in her tracks by the sight that confronted her. She had left a group of peaceful, deserted Sunday premises. The place now looked as though all hell had broken loose. There was a fire engine and uniformed figures running purposefully about. People were gathering to watch from across the road.

A car screeched past her, skidded to a halt, and someone hurtled out of it and ran towards the centre of activity. It was only then that she realised, with a wave of hot panic, that the focus of all this attention was her shop.

Almost simultaneously it dawned on her that it was Hugo's car that had ended up slewed sideways behind the fire engine. Hugo was throwing a vicious punch at the fireman who was trying to stop him getting near the shop, and in another split second was having his arms pinned behind his back by a second fireman.

'We're here to fight the fire, mate, not you. Calm down,' she heard the man say authoritatively, drowning Hugo's impassioned shouting of her name.

She broke into a run and halted behind the heaving group.

'Hugo—I'm here,' she said loudly.

He spun round, and the firemen, feeling the aggression go out of him and realising that the danger was over, disappeared quickly to get on with their real work.

For a second Hugo stared at her as though he were seeing a ghost, then he was crushing her in his arms with a great, shuddering sigh.

'Oh—Petra! I thought you were in there. And the fools wouldn't let me get to you.'

The pain of his embrace was nothing to the sweetness of the knowledge it seemed to bring that he actually cared about her. She clung to him for a wild, indescribably blissful moment.

'Move away, please, sir, madam.' Hands were pulling them back. 'Right away, across the road, please. You're obstructing us in our work.'

'Where *were* you?' Hugo asked passionately as they broke apart, following immediately with, 'I'm not joining the gallows-watchers over there. Come down here.' He walked her back down the lay-by a little way, and put his arm round her shoulders as they stood against his car. 'Thank God you're safe!' he said, his grip tightening. 'Someone who knew me saw smoke and flames at the back of the shop, and called the brigade then me. I came quickly enough because of the property, but, when I saw lights still on upstairs and down in your place, I nearly went mad thinking you were trapped in there. Look at it!'

They stared at the awesomely transformed frontage of Collections. The door had been broken in, as had the top-floor windows. Smoke was pouring out, and there was the livid red of flames at the back of the shop. Water was thundering in now from the hose.

'Where were you?' Hugo repeated.

'Down the road, taking empties to the bottle bank. Then I sat in the park—I don't know how long for—and came back the long way round by Pemberton Road. How did it all start? I can't believe it. I can't have been away more than half an hour at the most.'

Hugo gave her a grim look. 'A lot can happen in half an hour.'

The spectacle had hypnotic fascination. The thought of the damage that was being caused inside the shop by both fire and water was horrific, silencing them both while the spasmodic shouts of the firemen rang out against the thunder of water and the hiss of steam.

'I can't think how it happened,' Petra said again bemusedly.

'What about your stock?' Hugo asked suddenly.

'It's all out in the van at the back. But never mind that. What about your premises?'

'We'll just have to wait and see.'

Someone was coming towards them. 'Mr Baron, isn't it?' he asked. 'I remember you from the fire check we did on these premises last year. John Carver, Chief Fire Officer.'

'Of course. How's it going in there?' Hugo gestured towards Collections.

'We've got it under control now, sir, or I wouldn't be here talking to you. It looked worse than it is. No risk to the adjoining premises.' He looked at Petra. 'You're the young lady causing all the concern, I take it? You were working in the shop, I believe?'

'Yes.' Hugo's arm had dropped from her shoulder now, and there was a gap between them.

'Were you using anything that could have led to the fire? The stove, for instance?'

'No, nothing.'

'You hadn't been smoking?'

'I don't smoke.'

The hose was turned off, and in the comparative silence a voice called, 'That's it, John. All clear.'

'Right!' the fire officer returned, then looked at Hugo again. 'We'll have to seal the premises, sir, until our fire-investigation team have a chance to go over the place in the morning. I don't think there'll be much damage to the fabric of the building apart from the woodwork in the kitchen doorway and the bottom of the stairs to the upper floor. But you can say goodbye to your fittings, of course, I'm afraid. There would be things of yours in there, miss?'

'No. I'd got everything out. I'm moving away,' Petra said.

'That's very lucky for you, isn't it?' The two men were looking at her, and suddenly the implication of the fire officer's questions struck home.

'You surely don't think——?' she began, but the words bunched in her throat and almost choked her at the enormity of the thought. 'You said an investigative team would have to come in?'

'To check that there's no suspicion of arson,' the fire officer said dispassionately, looking steadily at her. It was said now. The word made tangible.

Her eyes went to Hugo. His face was expressionless, without colour under the bleaching effect of the street-lights, but as he looked back at her she thought she saw anger dawn in his eyes.

'I presume Miss Collins can go?' he asked coldly, turning to the fire officer.

'Certainly, sir. As long as the young lady feels competent to drive.'

'I shall, of course, drive her home.'

'There's absolutely no need for that. I'm perfectly capable,' Petra protested.

Hugo looked scathingly at her. 'You look as though you could drop. I'm not having you risk mowing down half Cheltenham.'

Petra turned blindly and walked along to the end of the Row and round to the back where her van was waiting, leaving him having a final word with the fire officer. He was *not* going to drive her home.

They suspected her of deliberately starting the fire. The fire officer suspected her because it was his job to do so. But Hugo? Could Hugo really think that she would do something so despicable? Had their relationship really seemed the kind that would lead to so evil a final gesture? How could he think such a thing of her?

She remembered the way he had crushed her to him in relief that she was not in the shop. She was beginning to see now how much she had over-estimated the nature of his relief. It was not relief about her as a special person. He would have been just as glad that anyone on earth had not been trapped by fire in his premises. And how short-lived his relief had been. The next moment he had been capable of seriously thinking that she might have started the fire deliberately.

She had only been driving a short time when she realised that she could see Hugo's car in her rear-view mirror. He was tailing her home. What did he think she was going to do? Make a run for it? Her mouth tightened. She braked steadily—she didn't want to be responsible for wrecking his car as well—and when both vehicles had stopped she got out and so did he.

'Why are you following me?' she said angrily. 'I'm not going to do a moonlight flit. I'm going straight home.'

'And I'm making absolutely sure you get there.' There was crushing determination in his voice.

'No, you're not.' Her resolve matched his. 'I shan't move another inch until you drive off in your own direction.'

'Don't be so stupid,' he said. 'Get back in your van and drive on, you ridiculous woman.'

She folded her arms, looked studiously away from him along the road, and tapped her foot impatiently.

He walked briskly back to his car, fooling her completely. In two seconds he had locked the Alfa Romeo, come back to hoist her up like a sack of potatoes, and carried her round, kicking and pummelling at him, to dump her into the passenger-seat of her own van.

'And don't try to jump out,' he thundered, getting into the driving seat and slamming the door. His knees were up under his chin almost in the confined Petra-sized space. 'Damned gimmicky box on wheels,' he snarled. 'Keys?'

She didn't speak, and he snatched at her hand, prising open her fingers to extract the keys. The van engine started up—not the smoothest of starts—and they screeched off down the road.

'Your car's on double yellow lines,' she told him with satisfaction.

'Tell me something I don't know.'

'They'll tow it away, I expect.'

'They can blow the damned thing up for all I care right now.'

The street-lights flashed past at an alarming rate.

'And you'll be done for speeding if we live long enough,' she persisted.

'Do me a favour. Shut up.' He made no reduction in speed and the cargo in the back rocked as they lurched into Hob Lane, then box cannoned into box as they stopped in front of Oak House. Petra wondered wildly if she had used enough packing material for her precious bygones, then the next instant thought, What the hell does it matter?

Hugo came round and yanked the van door open. 'Out!' he ordered.

'You're not coming——' she began.

'I'm coming in. I've things to say to you.'

There was nothing she could achieve against him in this mood. He came in.

Her ready-packed suitcases were standing in the sitting-room. He pounced on them with a snarl, and while she watched, with all the hypnotised fixation of a rabbit confronting a stoat, he opened them one by one and dumped the contents on the floor.

'What are you *doing*?' she managed to squeal at last. 'Are you mad?'

He turned to face her, his eyes wild, his chest heaving.

'Yes, mad!' he roared. 'Stark, raving mad, and I can't do a thing about it. You're not going away, do you hear? I won't let you. Damn it—in spite of everything I've said, and in spite of that exhausting, emasculating fight I've put up against you—I'm going to have to bloody well marry you!'

There was an electric, sizzling silence while they stared at each other. Then hysteria bubbled up in Petra and would not be stopped. She began to laugh, uncontrollable laughter that took her over with frightening force. She collapsed on to the sofa, and the laughter became equally wild tears.

Hugo flung himself down on his knees and scrunched her into his arms, burying his head in her neck.

'Don't, Petra. Petra, darling, please don't!' Gradually his whispered words and soothing hands calmed her until she was still in his arms, only the occasional shuddering gulp shaking her.

'I didn't set fire to your shop, Hugo,' she said unsteadily.

'Of course you didn't.'

'He wondered if I had—that fire officer.'

'Routine procedure. I could see what you were thinking, but you can't argue with a chap who's just put a fire out for you. Why are we talking about this?'

'We must. I know what started the fire. At least, I think I do. The kettle blew itself up. It must have started there, in the wiring.'

He kissed her, the most gentle, silencing kiss imaginable. Then he looked at her with tenderness she had never expected to see in his eyes. 'Better now?'

She nodded.

'Sure? You're really all right?'

'Yes.' She gulped again, looking at him. 'Am I going mad, or was—was that a proposal?'

A rather shamefaced smile lit up his face. 'I'm not surprised you have to ask. But yes, it was. It is.'

A bubble of laughter came rippling up in her again. 'It would win a prize for originality.'

He gave her a little shake. 'Never mind the originality. Let me have an answer.'

She looked at him, head on one side, blue eyes slightly pink-rimmed but dancing with teasing joy. 'You made more of a statement. It didn't seem to require an answer.'

'Petra!' He shook her again.

'Well, let me see, then. You said—what was it? ''I'm going to have to bloody well marry you!'' I think an appropriately romantic answer would be: I'm going to have to bloody well let you!'

He gave a shout of triumphant laughter and pulled her to her feet, then the laughter ended as he took her firmly in his arms and kissed her long and satisfyingly.

He sighed into her hair. 'I couldn't bear the thought of your going away. I did all I could to stop you, but I fought against the ultimate way of keeping you here. It was only tonight when I thought you might die that I knew what a fool I'd been.' He looked into her eyes, all barriers down. 'I knew then that I couldn't live without you, whatever might happen.'

She reached up to kiss him again. 'And what exactly do you think might happen?'

He studied a moment. 'I expect, judging by the way things have been so far, that we'll fight now and again.'

'But think of the making up!'

'Then there's Alexander. Things have to be right for him.'

'Of course. We'll make sure they are. I tell you here and now, Hugo Baron, that I consider Alexander a bonus. You might say he's one of the prime inducements to marry you.'

'And there's my mother. She has a habit of telling people what to do. I haven't managed to cure her of it in thirty-five years. She has told me unceasingly that if I had a grain of sense I'd grab you before somebody else did.'

'So where's the problem? Your mother says things I agree with.'

'But, most important of all, there's your "seize the moment" philosophy.' He looked at her with intense seriousness. 'I warn you, Petra, if you ever feel like seizing any chance to go away from me, I'll be right after you. I'll drag you back, kick and scream how you will. This is for keeps.'

'What other way would I want it?' She hugged him ferociously. 'Hugo Baron, don't you know that I only want to spend every living moment with you, now that you've given me the opportunity—the biggest opportunity I've ever had the chance of seizing?'

Words melted into action until Hugo reluctantly let her go.

'Time to be off. My mother stayed on with Alexander. She'll be wondering what on earth's happened.' He grinned with satisfaction. 'Oh, boy! Am I going to enjoy telling her!'

'You're forgetting something,' Petra said. 'You can't go unless I take you. And you may not have a car to go to.'

'Well, of course you're taking me!' he said in a lordly way. 'And, whether my car's there or not, you're coming over to Abbotswood to do the telling with me. Then you're staying on so that we can tell Alexander first thing in the morning. That should give him one up on Nigel Forest, whose mother is decidedly on the plump and plain side, with no knowledge of the intricacies of marbles at all.'

Petra collected a few things together, happy to obey orders of such a pleasant kind. Outside in the darkness she paused before getting into the van and drew in a deep, satisfying breath.

'Smell the earth!' she said. 'They've been ploughing this weekend.' She pointed out the straight furrows lining the field opposite Oak House, making a regular pattern of light and shade under the silver moon. She thought of the railway lines she had so nearly accepted as her panorama, and breathed in again.

Hugo squeezed her waist. 'Like us, that field, in a way, isn't it?' he said. 'Think what a hard time the earth's been through, but oh, what a glorious harvest there's going to be.'

# Next Month's Romances

Each month you can choose from a world of variety in romance with Mills & Boon. Below are the new titles to look out for next month, why not ask either Mills & Boon Reader Service or your Newsagent to reserve you a copy of the titles you want to buy — just tick the titles you would like to order and either post to Reader Service or take it to any Newsagent and ask them to order your books.

| *Please save me the following titles:* | Please tick | √ |
|---|---|---|
| THE WIDOW'S MITE | Emma Goldrick | |
| A MATTER OF TRUST | Penny Jordan | |
| A HAPPY MEETING | Betty Neels | |
| DESTINED TO MEET | Jessica Steele | |
| THE SEDUCTION STAKES | Lindsay Armstrong | |
| THE GREEN HEART | Jessica Marchant | |
| GUILTY PASSION | Jacqueline Baird | |
| HIDDEN IN THE PAST | Rosemary Gibson | |
| RUTHLESS LOVER | Sarah Holland | |
| AN IMPOSSIBLE KIND OF MAN | Kay Gregory | |
| THE WITCH'S WEDDING | Rosalie Ash | |
| LOVER'S CHARADE | Rachel Elliot | |
| SEED OF THE FIRE LILLY | Angela Devine | |
| ROAD TO PARADISE | Shirley Kemp | |
| FLIGHT OF SWALLOWS | Liza Goodman | |
| FATHER'S DAY | Debbie Macomber | |

If you would like to order these books from Mills & Boon Reader Service please send £1.70 per title to: Mills & Boon Reader Service, P.O. Box 236, Croydon, Surrey, CR9 3RU and quote your Subscriber No:.........................................................(If applicable) and complete the name and address details below. Alternatively, these books are available from many local Newsagents including W.H.Smith, J.Menzies, Martins and other paperback stockists from 9th October 1992.

Name:.................................................................................

Address:.............................................................................

.................................................Post Code:.......................

**To Retailer: If you would like to stock M&B books please contact your regular book/magazine wholesaler for details.**

You may be mailed with offers from other reputable companies as a result of this application.
If you would rather not take advantage of these opportunities please tick box ☐

# WIN A TRIP TO ITALY

**T**hree lucky readers and their partners will spend a romantic weekend in Italy next May. You'll stay in a popular hotel in the centre of Rome, perfectly situated to visit the famous sites by day and enjoy the food and wine of Italy by night. During the weekend we are holding our first International Reader Party, an exciting celebratory event where you can mingle with Mills & Boon fans from all over Europe and meet some of our top authors.

## *HOW TO ENTER*

We'd like to know just how wonderfully romantic your partner is, and how much Mills & Boon means to you.

Firstly, answer the questions below and then fill in our tie-breaker sentence:

1. **Which is Rome's famous ancient ruin?**

   ☐ The Parthenon     ☑ The Colosseum     ☐ The Sphinx

2. **Who is the famous Italian opera singer?**

   ☐ Nana Mouskouri     ☐ Julio Iglesias     ☑ Luciano Pavarotti

3. **Which wine comes from Italy?**

   ☑ Frascati     ☐ Liebfraumilch     ☐ Bordeaux

Tie-Breaker:  Well just how romantic is your man? Does he buy you chocolates, send you flowers, take you to romantic candlelit restaurants? Send us a recent snapshot of the two of you (passport size is fine), together with a caption which tells us in no more than 15 words what makes your romantic man so special you'd like to visit Rome with him as the weekend guests of Mills & Boon.

..............................................................................................

..............................................................................................

..............................................................................................

..............................................................................................

**Mills & Boon**

In order to find out more about how much Mills & Boon means to you, we'd like you to answer the following questions:

**1. How long have you been reading Mills & Boon books?**

☐ One year or less ☐ 2-5 years ☐ 6-10 years

☑ 10 years or more

**2. Which series do you usually read?**

☑ Mills & Boon Romances ☐ Medical Romances ☐ Best Seller

☑ Temptation ☐ Duet ☑ Masquerade

**3. How often do you read them?** ☐ 1 a month or less

☐ 2-4 a month ☐ 5-10 a month ☑ More than 10 a month

---

Please complete the details below and send your entry to: Mills & Boon Reader Service, FREEPOST, P.O. Box 236, Croydon, Surrey CR9 9EL, England.

Name: .................................................................................................

Address: .............................................................................................

.................................................... Post Code: ...............................

Are you a Reader Service subscriber?

☐ No ☑ Yes my Subscriber No. is: ...................................................

---

## RULES & CONDITIONS OF ENTRY

1. Only one entry per household.
2. Applicants must be 18 years old or over.
3. Employees of Mills & Boon Ltd., its retailers, wholesalers, agencies or families thereof are not eligible to enter.
4. The competition prize is as stated. No cash alternative will be given.
5. Proof of posting will not be accepted as proof of receipt.
6. The closing date for entries is 31st December 1992.
7. The three entrants with correct answers who offer tie-breaker sentences considered to be the most appropriate and original will be

judged the winners.
8. Winners will be notified by post by 31st January 1993.
9. The weekend trip to Rome and the Reader Party will take place in May 1993.
10. It is a requirement of the competition that the winners attend the Reader Party and agree to feature in any publicity exercises.
11. If you would like your snapshot returned, please enclose a SAE and we'll return it after the closing date.
12. To obtain a list of the winning entries, send a SAE to the competition address after 28th February, 1993.

You may be mailed with offers from other reputable companies as a result of this application. Please tick the box if you would prefer not to receive such offers. ☐